Anonymous

Millionaires and How they Became so

Anonymous

Millionaires and How they Became so

ISBN/EAN: 9783337371173

Printed in Europe, USA, Canada, Australia, Japan

Cover: Foto ©Andreas Hilbeck / pixelio.de

More available books at **www.hansebooks.com**

MILLIONAIRES

AND

HOW THEY BECAME SO.

SHOWING HOW TWENTY-SEVEN

OF

THE WEALTHIEST MEN IN THE WORLD

MADE THEIR MONEY.

REPRINTED FROM TIT-BITS.

PRICE SIXPENCE.

London:

"Tit-Bits" Offices, 83, 84, & 85, Farringdon Street.

1884.

CONTENTS.

THE ROTHSCHILDS.

STEPHEN GIRARD (OF PHILADELPHIA).

SIR WILLIAM ARMSTRONG.

WARREN HASTINGS.

JOHN RYLANDS (OF MANCHESTER).

SIR JOSIAH MASON (THE PENMAKER).

SIR GEORGE ELLIOTT ("THE BONNIE PIT LADDIE").

J. W. MACKEY (OF CALIFORNIA).

JAMES YOUNG (OF GLASGOW).

JOSEPH PEASE.

CONTENTS.

JAMES BAIRD

(THE SCOTCH IRONMASTER).

ROBERT NAPIER (OF GLASGOW).

GEORGE MOORE (THE DRAPER).

CONCLUSION.

MILLIONAIRES

AND

HOW THEY BECAME SO.

UNDER this heading we publish the history of certain great fortunes. We do not propose to preach the " gospel of greed," but rather to tell the method of success. Every true man has a laudable desire to become rich. In our efforts to assist our reader to accomplish this end, we shall not repeat the well-worn precepts that are dinned into the ears of every well-trained young man. We shall give the actual methods by which colossal fortunes have been accumulated.

No doubt much of the wealth that has been gathered into single hands has been got by doubtful schemes. But that will not deprive it of its interest, and may serve as a warning to others.

The following list of all British fortunes exceeding a quarter of a million personalty, which have been transferred by death within the last decade, may be of interest at the outset of these articles: Sir David Baxter, ironmaster, Dundee, £1,098,000; Baron Wolverton, Lombard-street, £1,000,000; Mr. T. Baring, banker, 8, Bishopsgate Within, £1,500,000; Mr. E. R. Langworthy, Manchester, £1,200,000; Mr. Joseph Love, Durham, £1,000,000; Mr. James Baird, Cambusdoon, Ayrshire, £1,190,000; Mr. J. P. Heywood, Liverpool, £1,900,000; Mr. John Penn, Lee, Kent, £1,000,000; Earl of Dysart, 34, Norfolk-street, Strand, £1,700,000; Mr. R. Thornton, Streatham Hall, Exeter, £1,000,000; Mr. Crawshay, Cyfarthfa Castle, Glamorgan, £1,200,000; Baron L. N. de Rothschild, 148, Piccadilly, £2,700,000; Mr. J. R. Mills, Kingswood Lodge, Tunbridge, £1,200,000; the Duke of Portland, Cavendish Square, £1,500,000; Mr. J. Williams, Caerhayes Castle, Cornwall, £1,600,000; Mr. Thomas Wigley, Timberhurst, Lancashire, £1,300,000; Mr. E. Mackenzie, Fawley Court, Bucks. £1,000,000. The following names, besides those mentioned in the above list, are given: Sir T. Beckett, Bart., Somerby Park, Lincoln, £350,000; Mr. F. Wright, Osmanton Manor, Derbyshire, £700,000; Sir Edmund Beckett, Bart., Doncaster, £300,000; Lady S. K. des Vœux, Drakelowe Hall,

Derby, £250,000; Mr. A. R. Strutt, Makeney, Duffield, Derby, £900,000; Mr. W. Herrick, Bean Manor Park, Leicestershire, £800,000; Earl Howe, Gopsall Hall, Leicestershire, £250,000; Mr. Edward Tew, Crofton Hall, Yorks., £600,000; Mr. George Wolstenholm, Kenwood Park, Sheffield, £250,000; the Earl of Shrewsbury, Alton Towers, Staffs., £350,000; Mr. James Brown, Rosington, Yorks., £250,000; Sir Titus Salt, Crow Nest, Halifax, £400,000; Mrs. Frances H. Miles, Firbeck Hall, Yorks., £350,000; Mr. Charles Cammell, Derby, £250,000; Mr. George Hadfield, Sheffield, £250,000; Mr. John Foster, Bradford, £250,000; Mrs. Vernon Harcourt, Swinton Park, Yorks., £250,000; Mr. Thomas Cross, Ruddington Hall, Notts., £350,000; the Hon. Augustus Duncombe, Dean of York, £500,000; Mr. Alfred Harris, Oxton Hall, Yorks., £300,000; Sir R. Burdett, Bart., Foremark, Derbyshire, £300,000; Mr. Joshua Appleyard, Halifax, £300,000: Mr. Mark Firth, Oakbrook, Sheffield, £600,000; Mr. John Thorpe, Elston Hall, Notts., £380,000.

We do not, however, confine ourselves to British millionaires, and our first sketch therefore will be an account of

JAY GOULD'S FORTUNE.

JAY GOULD, one of the American railroad kings, has just retired from business with a fortune of 100,000,000 dollars. He is, perhaps, the wealthiest man in the world. Although only 47 years of age, he has made more money than the Rothschilds, and he has done it in 25 years. While it has taken the wealthy Jewish house more than a century to acquire their millions, this man has done it in a few years by his own efforts.

Jay Gould's father was a struggling farmer near Roxbury, in the State of New York. At twelve years of age, Jay was sent from home with the cutting remark, "Go; you are good for nothing on the farm." He was given a suit of clothes and two shillings, and left to make his way in the world. While studying at the town school, he worked for a blacksmith in the evenings, in return for his board.

At fifteen, he was a partner in a business, and, after a few months, became sole manager. Not content with such a slow business, he put his father in as manager, and flew for higher game. By working night and day he qualified himself as surveyor and civil engineer, and soon had a corps of surveyors all over the State working for the Government. It was here he first showed his wonderful ability as an organiser and manager of men. Though only eighteen, he was doing the work of a mature man of forty. But his ambition was more than his strength. The illness that seized him nearly proved fatal. He, however, recovered, and continued the race for wealth. A new railway was just finished through the forests of eastern Pennsylvania, where there were large belts of hemlock trees. Gould bought a tract of land, and determined to start a tannery, and use the hemlock bark for tanning. This was the beginning of his wonderful career. From this time he never turned back. He had no capital, was merely a boy, had never worked in a tannery, and had no great things to recommend him, yet he boldly made advances to the largest tanner in New York. Such was his power of convincing others that he soon completed a partnership, and the tannery was in full operation 100 days after.

The town of Gouldsboro' was built near the tannery. All the town lots were sold by Gould. The bank was controlled by him. The post-office owned him as master, and the highways to town were built and owned by him. He was designer, creator, preserver, and king over that district. Nothing was bought or sold that did not in some way pay toll to him. In three years he was able to buy out his partner, and was then worth 100,000 dollars.

In 1860 Mr. Gould displayed for the first time that self-reliance for which he has since become so renowned. In a dispute with his then partner, who had seized on the tannery in his absence and was managing it to suit himself, Mr. Gould resorted to force as the quickest and cheapest way of carrying his own point. He selected fifty men and divided them into two companies, and stormed the tannery in front and on the roof. Every man was armed with a six-shooter, and the bullets whistled around like hailstones. Gould's party soon effected an entrance, and threw the defenders out of the upper windows. Having turned out his partner Gould resumed possession, and soon got the sole ownership.

The money made by this tannery venture was merely used as a stepping-stone to his great railway manipulations. The Erie Railway, then the greatest line in America, was sold under foreclosure of a mortgage, and Gould stepped up to buy a lot of its shares at the greatly reduced price. He saw that the railways of America were still in their infancy, and such a magnificent trunk line was destined to play an important part in the future development of the country.

He bought a majority of the shares, ingratiated himself with Daniel Drew, the president of the railroad, and soon was the controlling spirit of the company. In 1867 he caused a lot of fresh shares to be issued by the Erie Company, which were sold to the eager public as fast as called for, until the amount of the original capital was doubled. This is what was called "watering" the stock. There was no need for this. It was simply done to enrich himself and the members of the board. The sale of the shares produced 10,000,000 dollars, which was left as deposits in the various New York banks. And now came his greatest stroke of stock-jobbing. In the autumn, when all the money of the country was needed to pay for the crops, he and his partners suddenly presented cheques for the whole 10,000,000 dollars. It fell like a thunderbolt on the money market. Every banker called in his loans. This caused every stockholder to sell, and the prices of Erie shares fell from 80 to 35, at which price Gould bought all he could get. When he possessed all the shares that could be purchased he soon put up the price again until it touched 60 and 65, and netted by this one stroke a splendid fortune for a moderate man.

His wealth and his enterprise were by this time becoming a national theme. He stopped at nothing to accomplish his ends. Half-a-million dollars were distributed at the seat of the New York Legislature, and he got whatever Acts he wanted passed. A short line of railway, known as the Susquehanna, was needed to complete his system of monopoly. Instead of buying it in the ordinary way, he simply let it be known that it would have to be annexed whether the shareholders liked it or not. So, getting a warrant from Judge Barnard, in his own employ, he sent a man down by special train with an army of rowdies, all armed with guns and revolvers. Seizing the head offices of the road, he put in his own officials, and was proceeding to take possession of the trains as they came in, when he was suddenly interrupted by a force from Albany composed of railway men, led by a Mr. Van Valkenburg. Gould's train was thrown from the rails by a frog placed specially to disrail the engine. Gould's men and his sheriff, were captured by the Susquehanna crowd, and kept in close confinement, whilst Van Valkenburg and his increased army of over 1,000 men took a train to meet the fresh reinforcements they knew were coming to aid Gould. The two trains of opposing forces met near a long tunnel, and while Gould's engine whistled for " down brakes," the Susquehanna " boys " rushed with a full head of steam right on to their foes. The two engines came together with a frightful collision, but, as everyone saw what was coming, all jumped before the actual catastrophe. A party of militia from New York came providentially on the scene and stopped all further warfare, or many valuable lives might have been lost. As it was, dozens of men were badly wounded. Gould was successful, as usual, in the end.

The power exercised by Gould may be imagined. He controlled judges, courts, legislators, senators, sheriffs, newspapers, and railways. He now strove to control the money of the nation, and even looked toward buying up the very President himself. To do this he became acquainted with President Grant's brother-in-law, and through him obtained an introduction. A special steamer on the Hudson River and a grand pic-nic were organised, to which the President and his family were invited. Gould hoped at this grand pic-nic to learn the views of the General on the finances of the Government, and to impress on the people that he and General Grant were in one accord on the great financial questions of the day. He hoped to put gold up in price. He might as well have tried to open an oyster with a leaden spoon as to open the mouth of the sphinx-like President. Grant's only remark to Gould's many inquiries was that " there was a fictitiousness about the prosperity of the country, *which bubble might as well be burst now as any time."* When Gould and his satellites heard that remark they knew that the death-knell to their prosperity was sounded—at least to most of them. If gold were to fall the fictitious values to which they had forced their shares would all disappear, and they would be ruined. Bribes were freely offered to the gentlemen in immediate attendance on General Grant. Half-a-million in gold was placed to the credit of General Porter, who, it was hoped, would interfere to influence the mind of the President and cause the Secretary of the Treasury to cease from selling gold, so that it might keep up in price. General Porter refused the munificent bribe, and the price of gold began to fall.

One Wednesday night in September, 1873, gold had closed at 140. Jay Gould learnt at midnight that the President of the United States was determined to reduce the price to its legitimate value. He saw the whole extent of the danger to himself : he knew the ruin a Treasury sale would bring to him, so he made up his mind to leave all his friends in ignorance and sell as quietly and rapidly as he could. Early on Thursday morning he engaged brokers to influence his friends to buy, and another lot of brokers he hired to sell for him. That afternoon gold was at 144. 239,000,000 dollars was the amount of transactions that day in the gold room. The attention of the world became fixed on Jay Gould and his doings. All business ceased for days. The exporting houses put their goods aside ; the importing houses left their wares in bond. From every quarter of the world gold was hastening to New York. The banks of England and France felt the drain, advices being telegraphed of millions at a time. Never had such a spectacle been seen by commerce—gold was flowing by streams and rivers to one spot, all to be poured down the capacious maw of one man. A Cabinet meeting was held in Washington, to which the President and his officers had come great distances at the call of the whole business men of the country. The nation was represented as on the brink of the greatest panic the States had ever seen. The papers were calling for the blood of the " arch-conspirator," and as he read the paragraphs speaking of a lamp-post and a rope, with a short shrift, he only smiled grimly. The little man who was making all this commercial earthquake is a thin, pale-faced, silent man, with black whiskers. He is a nervous, sensitive little fellow, with a determination to succeed. Amid all the tumult he quietly keeps his head cool, and adds a few more millions to his "pile." He advised Mr. Speyer, a German broker, to buy up all the gold that was offered at any price up to 160. In a few hours Speyer had bought 40,000,000 dollars worth, and he knew the supply was still increasing. The telegraphs were so crowded by messages that some of them actually melted with the heat of the continued current. Speyer was threatened on the Exchange with death if he did not cease to bid for gold, and in the excitement he went raving mad.

As soon as the Government began to sell, the price went down from 160 to 130 in fifteen minutes. In the midst of the ruin, surrounded by his dumbfounded colleagues, all stunned and broken down, sat the imperturbable Gould. The door of his office was protected by prize-fighters, armed with six-shooters.

He emerged from the chaos a wealthier man. All his partners were ruined. Poor Speyer went mad, Jim Fisk was shot, Tweed died in gaol, Judge Barnard was disgraced, deposed, and died of shame, and everyone connected with him was bankrupt. He used their corpses to bridge over the chasm of ruin, for himself to cross by.

But the world soon forgot all this. The glamour of his gold dazzled the eyes of the people of the West, and the very papers that were cursing him in '73 for bringing such desolation on their country, soon were encouraging the people to vote money and lands to help him to build his Wabash Railway, the finest system in the West. To-day his son is president and virtual owner of a road reaching from the Mississippi to the Atlantic.

BUDGETTS,

Of Bristol.

The firm of H. H. & S. Budgett, of Bristol and London, is probably the largest grocery house in the world. They own steamers and ships, and import their goods by the cargo. They employ clerks and warehousemen by hundreds, horses and carts by scores, and their dealings mount up into the million every year. Originally this firm kept a small grocer's shop in a dirty little colliery village called Kingswood.

The story of their success is not so exciting as some of the modern millionaires. But the methods of their rise and progress are the more interesting because they have every element of honesty and common-place practicability about them. Any man can do what the Budgetts have done. They have not invented any great labour-saving machine, nor gambled on the stock exchange, neither have they developed a new industry to startle and enrich the world.

From the most common-place of businesses, in the most insignificant village, and with scarcely any capital, they have risen to be merchant princes.

Their first step to fortune was the plan of offering "leading articles" at a low price to tempt new customers; then they were careful to retain every new customer by giving good value and good attendance.

Soon the village shop was besieged by the frugal housewives from the country round, who rode in on donkeys to make their purchases. The crowds of waiting customers suggested a system of small wholesale dealing, which really was the beginning of the house of the present day. Samuel Budgett went round on horseback to the little villages and took orders for the week's provisions from the villagers. His first " journey " was to the paltry hamlet of Pucklechurch. No doubt the substantial-looking travellers that now represent the house would look with contempt on any mention of a journey to Pucklechurch, but there the first journey for the princely house of Budgetts was taken.

As trade increased the ambition of the brothers expanded, and Samuel ventured on a more pretentious style of business, and here his secret of success best showed itself. He called upon the best grocers in one of the towns in Somersetshire, and offered to sell them goods wholesale. His reception was a decided rebuff—most of the best men advised him to go back home and mind his own business, and not come bothering them. Three or four such remarks as this brought out the stuff that he was made of. He told them with defiance that he had started out to do business, and do business he would: if they, the best shops, would not buy from him, he would sell to the small shops, their customers. This soon changed their views as to the man and his goods. He went home from his first extensive journey with the secret of a grand success in his head. The orders from that journey were the embryo cargoes that now are unloaded on the wharves at Bristol. Every journey was conducted on the same principles : if the larger grocers would not buy from him he supplied the small shopkeepers, their customers. In this way a growing trade was soon built up. He never lost a customer when once obtained. His principle was, that it is more important to retain a customer than to gain a new one.

The old-established houses in Bristol were astonished at the effrontery of a country shopkeeper in such a wretched village as Kingswood daring to call upon the same shops as they supplied.

The trade increased fast, travellers were engaged, and the journeys extended, until the connection covered the country for a hundred miles around. More men were engaged, more horses were bought, and the warehouses enlarged. At last premises were taken in Bristol.

The largest houses in Bristol saw the customers they had hitherto supplied buying in the same markets as themselves, and competing to sell to the same men. Envy, malice, and all uncharitableness assailed them on all sides. Rumours of their failure were freely set afloat, and a combination to ruin them was established. Without a word of warning every creditor suddenly presented his account for immediate settlement, many of them not being due. It was a trying time, but each received a cheque for the amount in full. Though the proceedings were irregular, Mr. Budgett decided that all should be paid. When the last cheque was given there was no cash in the bank to meet it, but by borrowing from a friend and riding on a swift horse the money for the amount was paid in at one counter of the bank just before the cheque was presented at another. Bankruptcy was avoided, and the Budgetts stood higher in the commercial world than before. Such a combination to destroy their credit could never have been met if they had sold goods on long credit. Most of their sales were for cash, and to this method of doing business the firm attribute their ability to stop all such attacks. A second attempt to ruin them was made, but it was as promptly met, and the originator made to apologise publicly.

More travellers were put on the road, larger warehouses were taken, and a London house established. But the same principles governed the business as when it was confined to the little shop. Family prayers were held every morning in the large warehouses, and all the workpeople and the partners with their sons were expected to be there at seven o'clock or pay a fine. The partners were fined half-a-crown, which the cashier duly collected if late, and the workmen a less amount, in proportion to the importance of their situation.

Budgetts were sneered at for their religion, and reviled for their punctuality, but their fair dealing attracted trade, and their promptness retained it.

Everything was moving along smoothly to a deserved success (Samuel, the younger brother, was now the sole proprietor in the concern) when a most disastrous fire burnt up the entire range of warehouses at Kingswood, containing full stores of sugars, teas, flour, coffee, cheese, butter, &c. In all about £13,000 worth was destroyed.

What would have been an irretrievable loss to many was merely a pause for a few hours to Samuel Budgett. The fire occurred at night. In the early morning, when the fire engines were still playing upon the smoking ruins, Mr. Budgett rented a large warehouse in Bristol, stocked it with goods, and next day business was running along much as usual, and all the orders were fulfilled. Soon the fine building which now graces the narrow little crooked Bristol street was erected, and from that time to this Budgetts have never looked back.

The leading spirit in this successful firm was Samuel Budgett. He was a little man of cool demeanour, with active, nervous temperament ; a grand judge of human nature, and having a clear eye to the "main chance." There were no "stores" in his time, nor was there any such system of advertising as is now in vogue. The course of trade ran along in the old grooves with a good margin of profit, and all kinds of subterfuges were in fashion to enhance the profits of grocers. No borough analysts visited shops with a view to detection. All kinds of adulteration and deception were practised. Teas were coloured, coffees were mixed with chicory and sold as genuine, sugars were salted, pepper was mixed with dust, mustard contained turmeric, and soap was weighted with clay. Mr. Samuel Budgett had been trained from his boyhood to look upon these things as fair dealings, and it was not until his success was beyond any doubt that he determined to do business on a better footing. But it paid, and paid big in the end, to do the honest thing with his customers. They discovered, after a while, that his goods were purer than most merchants, and it left them at liberty to adulterate for themselves if they chose to do it.

Samuel Budgett was naturally a religious man. It was as essential to him to be religious as it was to breathe. When in the zenith of his wonderful career he often walked miles to some paltry village chapel to officiate as local preacher. This gave his competitors a good handle to chaff about him "preaching for orders." It was said that every sermon was as good as an extra traveller. But the little man paid no heed to the satire. He did good, and it paid him.

Most of the employés were like himself, of a deeply religious turn, and he found it paid to have such men. His customers were better satisfied to be served by them, and he seldom was wronged by his men.

The people of Kingswood still tell a story of his kind way of dealing even with those who had cruelly wronged him. A young married man who had been with him some years was discovered in some malpractices, and was summarily dismissed. The young fellow foolishly tried to injure his late employer and ingratiate himself with other houses by traducing the stability of the Budgetts. The attempt to injure their credit was futile, the young man was exposed, and compelled to publicly apologise. His future was one continual struggle ; no one would employ so vindictive a man, and he eventually succumbed to the temptation of drink.   In a few years he returned to Kingswood with a small family, a sickly wife, and ruined constitution.   Without any character, and with bad habits, he was fast going to ruin, when Samuel Budgett happened to hear of his circumstances.   His arrears of rent were paid, his little furniture was released from the pawnshop, and after gaining his pledge to the temperance cause, he was helped to gain a situation.   That man became a worthy citizen of Bristol.

Instead of turning his back on the village where his money was made and removing to some fashionable place, he bought land in the little colliery town, and built a good house among his old neighbours.   The rude colliers of that day were benefited by his life and example.

But such energy as he displayed in all his undertakings, such anxiety, work, and over-activity told their tale on the little man. Though only fifty-five years of age his strength began to fail, his breath gave tokens of a heart affection.   He had been living too fast.   Just when the sun of prosperity was shining most brightly on his path, his health began to fail, dropsy of the heart set in, and soon the active spirit that gloried in exertion was laid to rest for ever.

MR. BRASSEY'S MILLIONS.

UNLIKE many millionaires, Mr. Brassey did not rise from nothing, for his father was a landed proprietor in Cheshire, owning about three hundred acres.

Thomas Brassey was born in 1805 at Buerton.   His school days at Chester were totally different from the school days of most wealthy men.   Instead of making small speculations out of his schoolmates by saving up his pocket-money and investing in sweet stuff to retail out at a big profit, he was one of the most open-minded, generous boys in the school.   There was no drying up of the milk of human nature in his case.

One of the great causes that enabled Mr. Brassey to accumulate his millions was the fact of his being such a universal favourite. Everyone liked him, and all trusted him.   When little more than a boy, he was sent by his employer to assist in the important work of surveying under the great engineer Telford.   When a mere youth, his master (a land surveyor) offered to take him in as partner, and at only twenty-one years of age he was full partner and exclusive manager of the Birkenhead branch of the firm.   At that time Birkenhead was a mere hamlet, but Thomas Brassey was agent for the greater part of the land where now stands the magnificent town by the Mersey. Brassey found ten houses in Birkenhead ; he lived to help to place in it ten thousand.

When only twenty-two years of age he foresaw the grand future of Birkenhead, and started limekilns and brickworks for himself. Liverpool was growing fast, and the demand for building materials was increasing. He had no difficulty in selling all he could produce, at good profits.

The times were in his favour. Railways were being introduced, and towns were developing fast. This was a time for men to lose their heads and, by rushing into rash speculations, swamp themselves in debt and despair. All kinds of " wild cat" enterprises were floated, and thousands of business men became bankrupt never to rise again. But young Brassey kept his course with unerring prosperity.

The Manchester & Liverpool Railway was then building under the direction of the great George Stephenson. This was the first passenger line that was ever constructed. Here was Mr. Brassey's' golden opportunity. He sought and obtained an introduction to the great engineer, and though only a yonng man, he so impressed Stephenson with his good judgment that he obtained the powerful friendship and help of the greatest engineer of his time.

This friendship was really the first stepping-stone to his future great wealth, for it was by George Stephenson's advice that he made his first tender for a contract.

The character of the man was shown in that first tender. Although but a youth there was no boyish display of rashness, no under-bidding for the sake of obtaining a contract. Young Mr. Brassey's tender was several thousand pounds higher than the lowest one, and the care shown in this effort so convinced his bankers of his conservative character, that they voluntarily offered to lend him a large sum to carry on his contracting work for the future.

It is impossible for anyone, at the present date, to conceive of the difficulties that were in the way of organising an army of untrained navvies. The work was new, not merely to himself, but to everyone. All the best methods of working had to be developed as the contract proceeded. The contractor with the greatest resources and the most ingenuity was the one who would make the biggest profit. Thomas Brassey soon adopted a plan that enabled him to outstrip many of his competitors. He found that if he allowed his best workmen to sub-contract for a small portion of the work it would save him many overlookers, and would hasten forward the business. The only workmen he could obtain were farm labourers or town mechanics; there were no trained navvies nor skilled foremen to direct them. There were no railways to bring up supplies and men. Everything was brought by waggon, and the great difficulty was in rapidly moving the large army of men from place to place. These difficulties were all surmounted, and every undertaking that Mr. Brassey contracted for was quickly dispatched and thoroughly done.

The eminent Locke, the next greatest engineer to George Stephenson, soon discovered that all Mr. Brassey's contracts were executed promptly and well, and little or no supervision was needed where he did the work. Brassey's great aim was to be true to his word.

When he and Mackenzie were building a railway in France under the direction of Locke, a magnificent viaduct, nearly a quarter of a mile long, suddenly collapsed. It had cost £50,000, and was a great loss to him. He might have shuffled the responsibility, and wriggled out of the contract. But he manfully determined to stand to his word, and rebuild the great structure in a more substantial manner. This decision gave him such a standing in the railway world, that most engineers and most companies were anxious to get him to contract for work on their lines.

Thomas Brassey wasted no money on lawyers. His greatest dislike was to waste time, money, and patience in law courts. He said that many a bright future had been blasted in a lawyer's office.

In 1845, Mr. Brassey was the largest contractor in the world. He had works proceeding in all parts of the United Kingdom, and two or three places in France. Altogether he had nearly one thousand miles of railway in progress. In first starting on his career it was his rule to always superintend personally his great contracts. But now this was impossible. All the management was intrusted to agents, and in this matter of choosing agents Mr. Brassey showed the stuff of which he was composed. Seldom or never was he wrong in his opinion of a man. His clear insight into human nature helped him wonderfully in manipulating all his corps of men.

The confidence shown in Thomas Brassey seemed universal. Kings, governments, companies, capitalists, and labourers alike trusted him. He handled one hundred and fifty millions of other people's money, and no one ever lost a penny by him.

But the most trying time of his life occurred in 1866. He was a partner with the unfortunate firm of Morton Peto, Betts, & Co., that failed on the memorable day which started one of the worst financial crises that England has ever seen. Sir Morton Peto failed for several millions, and with his downfall many of the oldest firms in London were tottering to a crash. Universal distrust prevailed. Some excitable writers distrusted the Bank of England itself. Bankers were drawing in their loans. Merchants were calling for settlements, and interest rose to 12 per cent. on the best security. The Austro-Prussian war was in progress, endangering the peace of all Europe, and the minds of men were filled with the gloomiest anticipations. Many public works were closed, and thousands of workmen thrown out of employ.

Mr. Brassey was involved to the tune of £3,000,000 by a long series of uncompleted contracts, from none of which could he realise a penny until finished. He was paying £120,000 for interest on the shares of one railroad alone in Austria. He was disbursing £45,000 a-month for wages on the same contract ; yet on his millions of bonds taken in payment for work completed he could not borrow for less than 8 or 12 per cent.

On some of his contracts he was working at a dead loss. At Barrow and Runcorn he was losing £40,000 or £50,000. In Denmark he was heavily involved. At the Victoria Docks, London, his liabilities were over half-a-million.

Some of his contracts, like the Evesham one, were paid entirely in shares that were totally unsalable in the then condition of finances. His Polish works were paid in the same way, and the Queensland railway was yet uncompleted and unpaid for.

Mr. Brassey's disasters all came together. The key to his whole operations was in the Austrian railway. If that were finished by January, the date of the contract, his payment of the large amount (£120,000) for interest would cease, his disbursement of £45,000 a-month would stop, and the million and a quarter of bonds that he held could be sold for cash.

But the line of railway ran through the very battle-grounds of the Austrian and German armies, and the latter were anxious to stop all progress on the road. Several thousands of labourers were working at the end of the line, and their wages were due. If the money could not be got to them they would cease work and wander away, never to return. It was a perilous undertaking. A desperate case needed a desperate remedy. A journey of 500 miles from Vienna to Lemberg, through two armies of soldiers with a large amount of money, and over a newly-built railroad, was no child's play. It required unusual courage to run the risk of flying bullets, broken rails, and burnt bridges. But such was Mr. Brassey's influence over men that he inspired others with the rashness and daring that he himself possessed, and a Mr. Offenheim undertook to convey £40,000 by railway to the labourers in the interior.

Everyone seemed to conspire against his going. The minor railway officials declared that there were no engines to be got. The engine-drivers refused point blank to risk their lives, and no fireman could be got to undertake the journey.

This opposition only spurred Mr. Offenheim to a determination to go at any cost. He searched among the works and found an old disused engine that had been laid away under a shed. He then persuaded an engine-driver to accompany him on the promise of five hundred florins, and provision for life for his wife and children if he got killed.

The old engine went creaking and rattling over the rough road, and dashed ahead at the rate of fifty miles an hour while passing through the sentinels of the two armies. The very daring of the enterprise so startled the soldiers that few of them shot at the retreating engine. Sometimes a bullet came tearing through the carriage, but the main danger was from fear of rails being removed.

It was a frightful risk those two men ran, but not greater than the occasion demanded. If that money did not get to Lemberg, the works would stop. The Anglo-Austrian Bank might fail, Mr. Brassey would certainly fail, and with his failure would come a worse crisis than had ever yet been seen. The whole civilised world would feel it. From Queensland to Canada, from Denmark to South America, and from India to Brazil great public works would stand still, and hundreds of thousands be cast out of work, while business firms would fall like card houses.

But the two men arrived safely with the cash. The wages were paid, the line was pushed on more rapidly than ever, and the contract was completed in October—five months before the date fixed. Thomas Brassey's prestige was established, his million and a-quarter of bonds lying in the Anglo-Austrian Bank were salable, and the whole financial world breathed more freely.

Mr. Brassey's son, the present Sir Thomas Brassey, says of him : " My father, ever mindful of his own struggles and efforts in early life, evinced at all times the most anxious disposition to assist young men to enter upon a career in life. The small loans which he advanced for this purpose, and the innumerable letters which he wrote in the hope of obtaining for his young clients help or employment in other quarters, constitute a bright and most honoured feature in his life."

Some idea of the vastness of his operations can be gathered from the fact that he often had more men employed under him than many a general leads to battle. At one time he had 80,000 men in his employ in different parts of the world, and used seventeen millions of pounds as capital in completing his various contracts.

THE ROTHSCHILDS.

THE founder of the great house of Rothschild was born one hundred and forty years ago at Frankfort-on-the-Maine. His method of success is described in two words—thrift and integrity.

The Rothschilds are to-day the arbiters of the destinies of nations. They rule over kings. If their purse-strings are closed no great war among European nations can be carried on. In 1820 they had loaned to eight governments £120,000,000, and that sum fades into insignificance compared with their gigantic transactions at the present day. They have banks in every capital in Europe. The house is spread like a network over the nations; and it is no wonder that its operations upon the money market are felt tremblingly by every cabinet and every exchange. It is the most powerful syndicate that ever existed. From St. Petersburg to San Francisco, and from New York to Bombay, the prices of money and of produce are affected by the views of the Jewish money-lenders.

In a little narrow back street of the Hebrew quarter in Frankfort was started the small office which has developed into the gigantic firm of to-day.

Meyer Anselm Rothschild, the founder of the house, was educated by his parents with a view to being either a schoolmaster or a priest. But his inclination led him to enter a money-changer's office as book-keeper. By saving most of his salary he was able to start as a money-changer and exchange-broker on his own account. It was slow, hard, up-hill work, and once or twice the little shop was nearly closing for want of business. But the strict honesty of the proprietor ultimately resulted in a gradually increasing business connection. In a few years he became known as the "honest Jew," and his thorough trustworthiness at last coming to the ears of the Landgrave of Hesse Cassel, he was occasionally employed by that potentate to do business for him.

While Buonaparte was devastating Europe with his vast armies, the Landgrave of Hesse Cassel found it paid him to sell his subjects as mercenary soldiers to the British and Prussians. In this way he accumulated over eight hundred thousand pounds sterling. This was all in silver, and difficult to remove.

The republican army of France, led by Napoleon, was marching against Frankfort to punish the Landgrave for his assistance to their enemies. He fled, and in his hurry he had no time to hide his silver, and to take it with him was impossible. To the honest money-changer in the narrow street he turned in his dilemma.

There was no time to waste. The outposts were coming in in breathless haste, proclaiming the rapid march of the invincible army. All was consternation in the city. The prince, who had sold his subjects as mercenaries to foreign powers, had no army to defend him, and flight was inevitable. Already the banners of the enemy were seen from the walls, and soon the legions would be thundering against the gates.

The Landgrave could save his life by disguise and flight, but his wealth must be left behind. He sent for Rothschild, and offered him the use of the whole free of interest if he would hide it from the French.

This was the golden moment in the history of the Rothschild family. If the custody of that million had been refused, the course of history would have been changed, and the house that has three times saved the peace of Europe would have been unknown to history.

The loan was accepted; but the removal of so large a sum amid the disturbances of a threatened siege was a risky undertaking. By the help of his friends Rothschild dug a hole in his garden, and at night proceeded to hide the wealth. He ran the double risk of being murdered by the people of the city for his money, or being shot by the French for hiding wealth. The task was scarcely completed as the soldiers marched through the city's gates and commenced their work of plunder. The banks and money-brokers were robbed of their all. His own property he did not conceal, for this would have occasioned a search; cheerfully sacrificing the less for the greater. He re-opened his office as soon as the town was quiet again, and re-commenced his daily routine of calm and steady industry.

He knew too well the use of money to allow the silver to lie idle in his garden. He dug it up at night time as he could use it to advantage, and made such handsome profits upon its use that on the owner's return, in 1802, he was prepared to refund the whole, and still have sufficient capital for his business. It was a time of war among the nations. Every ruler was wanting money and prepared to pay a high rate of interest for it. Rothschild extracted the last drop of blood from the borrowers who flocked to him, and they in turn squeezed the taxes from their poor down-trodden subjects. That system has been perpetuated to the present day. Every workman in Europe pays toll to the house of Rothschild, and so it will continue while wars shall last; and money-lenders fatten on the lifeblood of the people.

The refunding of the loan was not accepted. The Landgrave left it with the " honest Jew" for twenty years longer, at the nominal rate of two per cent. interest, and used his influence besides with the allied sovereigns, in 1814, to obtain business for Rothschild in the way of raising public loans. The Government of England employed him as agent for the payment of £12,000,000 to her German allies during the wars with Napoleon. This was the first great transaction of the Hebrew house, and it left a splendid profit in their hands. By this time the five sons of Meyer Rothschild were grown up to man's estate, and three of them were joined with the father in his banking house.

Rothschild united caution with boldness; he was the personification of the Yankee maxim, "Be sure you're right, then go ahead." The loans contracted by the firm during the great wars with France were always successful. No doubtful loan was accepted, and hardly any good loans were permitted to fall into other hands.

There was not room in Frankfort for the five sons and the father. It became necessary for some of them to seek other fields for their capital and industry.

Nathan, the second son, was dealing in English goods, and bought from a large wholesale trader who visited Frankfort regularly. This man had the whole of the trade to himself, and acted as though he were conferring a favour on the buyers by selling to them.

Nathan Rothschild offended him by not sufficiently acknowledging his greatness, and during one visit he refused to show Nathan his patterns. The high-handed dealer thought to ruin his customer. It was a fatal mistake.

The refusal to supply goods to Nathan was the second step in the upward course of the great house; it was on a Tuesday that the refusal was made; on Wednesday Nathan asked his father for a loan of £20,000, and on Thursday he started for England to buy his own goods, and to supply wholesale. The nearer he got to England, the cheaper he found the goods, and when he reached Manchester he discovered that things were about 50 per cent. cheaper than in Frankfort.

In Manchester he found that there were three profits—the raw material, the dyeing, and the manufacturing. He approached a manufacturer and offered to supply him with the raw material and the dye, and he should supply Rothschild with the manufactured goods. By this means he secured three profits for himself, and still could under-sell other dealers in Germany. The wholesale man who had treated him with such disdain was now fain to buy from him.

In a very short time Nathan had made his £20,000 into £60,000, and had secured the unbounded confidence of his wealthy father.

While the British troops in Portugal were struggling against the French, and the Government had great difficulty in getting gold to pay them, an opportunity offered for Rothschild to make a handsome profit out of the necessities of the nation. The East India Company had £800,000 in gold to sell—Rothschild snatched it up; knowing that the Duke of Wellington would have to buy it at any price to pay his troops.

B

The Government sent for Rothschild, and offered to buy all the gold at a fair margin of profit for him, but he was obdurate. Nothing but a princely fortune would satisfy him if he parted with the gold. At length, the Government were driven to give him his price, and on that one transaction he realised what would be a fortune to a moderate man.

But all the profit from that transaction was not yet secured. When the Government had the gold, they could not get it to the troops, and Rothschild undertook the task for them. He sent it by private couriers through France, and he afterwards declared that transaction was the best piece of business he ever did.

While Napoleon was marching backward and forward through Europe, making and destroying thrones, and ordinary business houses were crumbling to dust, the Rothschilds were piling up money by the hundred thousand. Nathan, although the second son, was chosen by the five brothers head of the household. His bank was in London.

While Wellington and Napoleon were facing each other in Belgium, he had a series of special couriers at intervals, reaching from the two camps to London. Rothschild felt that the tug for mastery was at hand when the two lions of war should meet at Waterloo. He knew it was "a king-making victory," and on the issue depended his fortunes, if he could obtain earlier information than others.

Whether Baron Nathan sent Mr. Charles Fowler over to Belgium, or whether that gentleman was there on other business, is not known, but it is beyond doubt that the first news of the battle of Waterloo was brought to England by Mr. Fowler, who was an architect, and who afterwards built Hungerford Market, and obtained the first prize for a design for New London Bridge. Mr. Fowler communicated the news to Baron Rothschild several hours before it was known to the British Government. It is often said that the news was first brought by Baron Nathan himself, and that the knowledge of the result of the battle enabled him to lay the foundations of the present splendid fortunes of that great monetary house. Indeed, there is a tradition relating how for six hours the Baron stood upon a hill overlooking the battle-field, and watched with beating heart the various changes of the day ; how when the shades of evening were beginning to fall, and the roar of artillery had gradually ceased, and the smoke that all day had enshrouded the fearful scene like a funeral pall slowly lifted, the Baron saw the French army in retreat, and knew that victory had come not only to the British arms, but to him, the anxious spectator. The Baron's rapid ride to the coast, his frantic appeal to the fishermen, the increasing offers, till at length, tempted by the prospect of earning 2,000 francs, one of the fishermen agreed to risk his life in the attempt to cross the stormy channel, the sudden change from tempest to favouring winds, the onward rush from Dover to London as fast as fresh relays of horses could carry him—all the little details are told with dramatic effect, but with a minuteness that is in itself evidence of their fictitious origin.

Baron Nathan was neither the bearer of the news nor the founder of the fortunes of his house. His father, who died in 1812, had left a large fortune behind him, which formed the nucleus of their present wealth. What Baron Rothschild really did was to turn Fowler's information to such good account that he is said to have cleared £200,000 on the Stock Exchange by his knowledge.

Wars are the very lifeblood of their house. If the nations were at peace the governments would not need to borrow, and national debts would cease. Then interest would fall, and money-lenders would need to turn to other fields than usury for their fortunes.

But wars were once almost the destruction of the house of Rothschild. In 1848, when the people of Europe were throwing off the yokes of kings, and France was ignoring all the pile of debt that her rulers had accumulated, the Rothschilds were severely crippled. The depreciation in funds and securities alone caused them a loss of £8,000,000.

But the Rothschilds soon recovered from that blow. The spirit of the father ever ruled the five brothers in their counsels. No great undertaking was ever attempted without consulting all the brothers. The spirit of the dead father may be said to direct to this hour the operations of his children. In every important crisis he is called into their counsels; in every difficult question his judgment is invoked. On his deathbed he laid upon them the paramount duty of inviolable union. This is one of the grand principles to which the success of the family may be traced. The co-partnership in which they were left has remained uninterrupted. Each of the brothers share equally in all results.

When wealth untold was secured, the brothers looked for titles among the sovereigns of the different nations. Austria conferred the appellation of Baron, and the brother in London was made consul-general of Austria. He afterwards was elected a member of Parliament, but was refused a seat because of his religion. His constituents returned him again and he was again refused. They elected him once more with the same result. Then, for the fourth time, they returned him, and Parliament no longer dared to turn a deaf ear to such a determined constituency. The oath was changed, and Baron Nathan Rothschild was the first Jew to sit in a British Parliament. He was a credit to his people and a worthy member of the House. He was honourable and very liberal in all his political views, and munificent in his charities.

As each successive generation is received into the partnership, and as each member usually marries a cousin, the wealth will remain among the family. Their immense wealth is being continually augmented by lucrative business. In time, the name will be more powerful and more lasting than many dynasties.

Fortunately, such power is generally used with moderation and discretion. Many of the ladies of the house of Rothschild have set splendid examples of charity in their liberal donations to the poor of other religions. The Baroness, in Paris, has endowed a large institution for the benefit of Christian poor.

Perhaps the greatest good that they have ever done to the world with their enormous wealth, was to help to build the railways across Europe. When other capitalists were timidly holding back from investing in the new enterprises, the Rothschilds stepped up with their millions and re-assured the less venturesome spirits, who gladly invested where they saw the Rothschilds were interested. To Baron James Rothschild, of Paris, is due most of the rapid development of the railways of Europe. He is reckoned the very first financier of the age. No great loan is ever issued by a government without consulting him.

A story is told of him that is quite characteristic of the man. During the outbreak of the Commune in Paris, a leader of Communists went to his office, and, during the interview, loudly declaimed against so much money being held by one man. He preached the doctrine of division.

"Well," said the Baron, "how much money do they say I am worth?"

"Sixty million francs."

"And how many people are there in France?" asked Rothschild.

"About forty millions," answered he of the Commune.

Handing him a pencil and piece of paper, he told him to figure out how much that was apiece.

"A franc and a-half each," said the man.

"Then there's your share. Now go, and don't come here again."

He went out with a puzzled look on his face.

STEPHEN GIRARD,

OF PHILADELPHIA.

SALAMANCA, the Spanish millionaire, complained that "Immortality can only be earned, it cannot be bought by riches." Statues of millionaires are scarce, but there is one to Stephen Girard that even a Shakespeare or a Wellington might covet.

In Philadelphia stands a colossal statue to a man who by his wealth was the saviour of a nation, a man whose wealth still rescues hundreds every year from poverty and crime. But he has a more enduring monument in the hearts of the people.

Yet he was a strange mixture of dishonesty and generosity, of harshness and self-denying charity. It is not the nine million dollars he accumulated that bought his fame, it is the noble disregard of his life during the yellow fever scourge.

Stephen Girard was born at Bordeaux in 1750. His father was a sea captain. At ten years of age, when he could barely read and write, he was turned out of home to make his way in the world as best he might. His first engagement was as cabin-boy on a vessel bound for the West Indies. Like all cabin-boys at that date, he was the football of the whole crew. He received more kicks than kindnesses, and among other rough usage was deprived of the sight of one eye.

Young, uneducated, friendless, wandering among strangers and partially blind; yet he only received ridicule for his misfortunes. This seems a hopeless beginning. But the lad had the right stuff in him to make a successful man. The chaffing he received for his blindness roused his temper, but did not subdue his spirits.

Everything made it difficult for him to fight his way in the world, but fight he did, and with successful results.

· He was a little fellow with broad, shoulders and a firm-set square jaw. Soon the pluck of the little lonely fellow began to have its effect on his mates, and from being the butt of the whole ship he soon became its idol, and eventually its master and owner.

Before he was out of his teens he had risen through the ranks of second mate, first mate, and captain. Then he got to be part owner, and eventually bought out his partners.

His ship traded mainly between the West Indies and American ports. From New Orleans he would take out flour, bacon, and general merchandise, and return with a cargo of fruit and vegetables. In his trading he was not merely captain and owner, but he was also merchant.

Money soon began to accumulate in his hands. At twenty years of age he had saved enough to retire from the sea. He opened a large store in Philadelphia and still made money. But in 1770 the War of Independence was raging, and all Girard's possessions were destroyed by it. His building was burnt with its stock of goods, and his trade was ruined.

He had to begin life again at the foot of the ladder. All the hard work of his past life was as good as thrown away.

His next venture was to buy claret from a French firm and bottle it; this proved a profitable business; in a few years he had saved enough to return to his old life. He bought a small ship, and re-commenced trading between New Orleans and the West

Indies. He was now thirty years of age; his wife had turned out a bad bargain—she was the daughter of a ship's carpenter in New York. Her eccentricity and want of sympathy seemed to make him morose and snappish. After ten years of misery with her, she developed into a maniac, and was incarcerated in a madhouse.

Girard now devoted himself exclusively to money-making. He shut his heart against all the pleasures of life, and devoted all his abilities to grubbing after wealth. He practised the most rigid economy. He did any kind of work to save money, and converted himself into a mere machine for collecting coin.

The starting-point for Girard's wealth was during one of the periodical insurrections in San Domingo. Two of his ships were lying in the harbour, when a sudden rush of citizens was seen to take place across the plaza, followed by a crowd of shouting blacks, gesticulating with maddened gestures, and threatening the handful of whites with guns and swords ; soon the noise of shots was heard, and the screams of terrified citizens were mingled with the shouts of the rebels.

The few half-castes that had started the rebellion were soon joined by thousands of others, and as every slave was promised his freedom if he revolted, the whole island was soon at the mercy of the mob. Merchants and planters were the main targets of the revolutionists—murder was the first step ; then robbery followed. Every wealthy inhabitant was anxious to save himself, his family, and his goods ; to do this, a hasty organisation was effected, and one of the officials elected leader.

The first skirmish with the insurgents convinced the wealthy whites that they were numerically too weak to compete with them. A scene of slaughter followed the attempt to escape. Men, women, and children were struck down in cold blood.

The ships in the harbour left for safety, and sailed for other ports. But Girard, who had seen so many revolutions, kept his ships close up to the pier, and armed all his men. When the other ships had left, he saw that his men were losing courage, and he knew that the only chance was to show a bold front if attacked. He threatened death to anyone who should show the white feather in an engagement, and promised rewards when the enterprise was over. He then waited for results.

A crowd of merchants and wealthy planters hurried down with as many of their treasures as they could carry. His ships were the only places of safety in the whole island. He promised to stay in the harbour until all had placed their goods and money on board. The people knew that the little dare-devil would be true to his word, and would defend his ships against all comers. Most of the richest people got their goods on board, and at night stole out to rescue their wives and children from their hiding-places. But many of them were caught and murdered before they could get back to the ships.

Girard waited in the offing until all chance of anyone returning was over. He then set sail for New Orleans, and carried the valuables as his cargo. No claimants were found, and he thus kept all as his own. This was a large haul for the daring captain. His few passengers were mulcted in a large sum for their rescue and passage to New Orleans.

This doubtful transaction was the initial point in the future millionaire's fortune.

He sold off his two valuable cargoes, and with the results he settled down in Philadelphia. As a merchant he throve, and soon started a bank.

In 1793 a terrible scourge of yellow fever broke out in the town. All who could fled in terror. Hundreds were dying of the filthy disease every day. There were no adequate means of isolating the sick. The few attendants who could be hired to nurse in the pest-houses soon died, and the dying were left untended. All the upper classes deserted the town, and the place was a pandemonium of lawlessness and death.

While the pestilence was at its worst a well-dressed gentleman of low stature and broad shoulders drove up in a private coach to the main hospital, where the most loathsome victims of the dreaded fever were collected. Not a nurse was left alive in the building. The dead were unburied, and no one dared to enter the charnel-house. Even the doctors had sickened, and many had died. But Girard, though one of the leading bankers of the country, left his business and entered the hospital to rescue some of the poor inmates.

He soon returned bearing in his arms a poor man suffering in the last stages of the fever. After placing the poor fellow in better quarters, Girard returned, and once more entered the hospital to act as nurse to the whole place. He almost lived amongst the patients, and gave both time and money to the grand object of a blessed charity.

He took upon himself the entire management of affairs, and in the dire necessities of the cases he performed the most menial services for the inmates.

He wrote to a friend at this time : " The deplorable situation to which fright and sickness have reduced the inhabitants of our city demands succour from those who do not fear death." For sixty days the banker left his business to nurse the sick with a woman's care and tenderness.

Five years after another visitation of the dreaded fever broke out, and again Girard devoted himself to nursing the sick.

This kindness and philanthropy did not hinder him from making money, in fact it assisted him in his business. The thousands of friends that he made by his self-denying charity published his business abroad better than any advertisement.

In 1812 he was rich enough to buy the old Bank of the United States, and commenced banking operations with a capital of over a million dollars. A great spirit of speculation was abroad in America, and Girard was the only banker who steadily set his face against it. He never bought an accommodation bill, and under no circumstances would he renew a promissory note. This secured him unbounded confidence, and when other banks were unable to meet their promises Stephen Girard stood as firm as a rock.

During the great war between the States and England, the credit of the American nation fell to a low ebb. The Governor at that time was anxious to borrow a large sum that was necessary to carry on the war to a successful issue. The volunteer armies of the States were doing battle manfully for their country, and the navy was carrying on a prosperous warfare, but the whole might be wrecked for want of funds. High rates of interest were offered, and various inducements held out to get the loan. But the capitalists of America were too heavily involved in their private businesses to render any assistance, even if they had sufficient foresight to see the grand future of their country.

At this juncture of affairs Stephen Girard stepped forward and placed the whole resources of his bank at the disposal of the Government. He proved the saviour of the nation. While all kinds of credit were shaken to their very centres, and the country was involved in difficulties arising from its exhausted finances and the expenses of the war, Girard not merely placed his all to the credit of the Government, but he raised loans and otherwise provided the "sinews of war" to support the men who were fighting for the existence of the nation. For five years he aided and supported the Government. In fact, he had thrown his weight in the scale, and he did not draw back until all danger was over.

When peace returned, and America was seated firmly among the nations of the world, he found his reward. All his advances were thoroughly secured, and his interest was faithfully paid.

Out of the 9,000,000 dollars which he saved, 2,000,000 were devoted to founding a college for orphans in Philadelphia. One of the rooms in the college is singularly furnished. When George Dawson visited it in 1874 he found that " all the plain, homely man's effects were shovelled into this room. Here were his boxes and his bookcase, his wig and his gaiters, his pictures and his pottery; and, hanging with careless grace, were his braces—old homely-knitted braces, telling their tale of simplicity and carefulness."

Most minute directions are left as to admission and management of the inmates. He specifically requires that the orphans be instructed in the purest principles of morality. As for religious belief, they are left to adopt such tenets as their mature reason may lead them to prefer; and to secure this he interdicts the employment and even the admission into the grounds of any ecclesiastic whatever.

SIR WM. ARMSTRONG.

ARMSTRONG'S works on the Tyne give employment to five or six thousand workmen; their weekly pay bill amounts to something like £10,000. The works themselves extend over fifty acres, and the whole town of Elswick is more or less dependent on these factories. They have a river frontage of over three-quarters of a mile.

One would naturally suppose that the man who had spent more than a quarter of a century in inventing the most destructive guns, would partake, more or less, of the character of a blood-thirsty desperado. It seems only reasonable to think that the man who has exhausted his genius in producing a widow-making and orphan-making machine, should be of the type of stage villain, with sinister look, black hair, and downcast eyes.

Armstrong is exactly the opposite of this. He is an open-faced, generous man, with a thoughtful cast of countenance, and bene-volent to a fault. His enormous fortune will probably be inherited by the public, as he has no children. Already he has devoted a magnificent park to his fellow-townsmen. Although he is known mainly for his inventions in gunnery, his fortune was started from other sources.

Half-a-century ago, in the wild, hilly districts of North York-shire, one day there stood a thoughtful youth, watching the waters of a mountain stream as they fell several hundred feet. He noticed that after spending most of their force in tumbling down the hill, they were utilised in turning a water-wheel at the bottom. Most of their force was exhausted, and only the remnant was made available.

The young man was a lawyer's clerk from Newcastle, spending his holidays in country rambles. It at once occurred to him that if the stream were conveyed from the summit in a pipe, and caused to act by pressure at the base, the whole fall, instead of a fractional part of it, would be made useful.

This was the starting point in the history of the man who is popularly supposed to be worth a couple of millions. The idea thus caught took deep root in his mind. He experimented for some time, and eventually perfected a hydraulic crane.

While he was thus spending his spare time inventing machinery, he was making his living in a lawyer's office. Armstrong was more of an inventor than a lawyer.

When the hydraulic crane was invented, the difficulty arose of getting a suitable opportunity for testing it. No one seemed to believe that anything could be done by a machine that had no wheels, or cranks, or steam, or handles. But a model was constructed and exhibited, demonstrating beyond dispute the new power of hydrostatics. It was determined to test the invention on the quay at Newcastle. Fortunately the new water-works of Whittle Dean had just been completed, giving the power of water that was needed to work the crane. The success was decisive. Armstrong now gave up the law, and turned mechanical engineer. Associating himself with some old friends, he started some small engine-works at Elswick. For years it was a struggling concern. The combined efforts of all the partners barely made both ends meet. Sneers were more plentiful than orders.

The great aim of the inventor was to get his hydraulic crane on the wharves at Liverpool. He knew that if he could get them at work there, it would be the best possible advertisement. Mr. Hartley was engineer to the port of Liverpool, and he was sceptical as to any crane being worked by mere water-power. At last he determined to visit Newcastle, and see for himself what the much-vaunted crane was able to do.

Mr. Hartley went down to the quay for the purpose of seeing it in full operation. He found it lifting hogsheads from the hold of a ship, under the direction of the keeper, who was known as "Hydraulic Jack." Mr. Hartley watched with astonishment the swift movements of the crane, which hoisted up the casks with great rapidity from the hold of the vessel, quietly swung round, and gently deposited them on the quay.

"You have got a queer machine; where are all the wheels?" said Mr. Hartley to Jack.

"There are none," answered Jack.

"But what makes it move?"

"It goes by water underground," replied the keeper.

"Do you ever let a hogshead fall?" asked the astonished engineer.

"Oh, yes," said Jack, "but I pick it up again before it touches the ground."

"You are not clever enough for that," said Mr. Hartley.

But Jack knew what the crane could do.

"What will you stand if I show you?" he asked.

Mr. Hartley never revealed how much he "stood," but it was sufficient to induce Jack to perform the following feat : Running a hogshead up to the highest point of the crane, he let it down with a rush that threatened to crush the cask into atoms, and caused Mr. Hartley to step suddenly back ; but Jack knew the power of the crane, and so dexterously checked the speed of the hogshead that it stopped within an inch of the ground.

" Wonderful, wonderful ! It's just the thing I want," exclaimed
Hartley, and hurrying off to Elswick Works he at once ordered
a couple for the docks at Liverpool.

This was the turning point in the history of the Elswick
factory. The recognition by the Liverpool authorities of the
excellence of the crane gave an impetus to trade, which had
hitherto been sluggish, and at once disburthened Armstrong's
mind of any apprehensions of future failure.

The invention of the hydro-electric machine was the second step
in the upward career of young Armstrong. While standing in
the boiler-house of a colliery near Cramlington, his attention was
called to a peculiar electrifying influence produced on anyone who
approached the steam that escaped from a fissure in the safety-
valve, through a cement of chalk and oil. This was the nucleus
of his second great invention. He found that it illustrated the
evolution of electricity during the conversion of water into
vapour, which, on an enormous scale, brings us nearer to the
phenomena of volcanoes and thunderstorms.

This invention was of little use in a monetary point of view, but
it introduced the inventor to the great engineers of his time, and
his fame began to spread through Europe. He was elected a
Fellow of the Royal Society, and from this time forward all his
claims for his discoveries and inventions were received with the
weight that his position carried. It was no longer a mere
provincial lawyer who asked for the attention of the scientific
world.

In 1854 the great struggle for mastery was taking place in the
Crimea. The resources of the four nations engaged were nearly
exhausted. A few masterful victories would decide the issue of
the great war. One terribly cold day in November, the battle of
Inkerman was progressing with varying fortunes. As regiment
after regiment was slain on either side, or exhausted by fighting,
fresh troops were brought up and the terrible slaughter continued.
The allied forces were fighting bravely to retain every foot of
ground, but the exposure to the severity of the storm, and the
greater numbers of the Russians, were slowly but surely driving
them back.

The British commander saw that unless something was done
before nightfall, he must relinquish his position. He had a couple
of eighteen-pounder cannon that would prove most effective
against the Russian artillery if they could be brought up. The
weight of each was two tons. The poor soldiers were exhausted
by the day's work, but he decided that the cast iron cannons must
be got into position at all cost. The great weight of the guns
rendered this a most dangerous and arduous undertaking. At last
they were brought into position, and poured their shot into the
Russian ranks with crushing effect. Their superior range soon

silenced the enemy's fire. The tide of victory was turned, and all by two cast iron cannons. The course of history was changed.

This incident led to the third cause of Mr. Armstrong's great fortune. On hearing of it, and knowing the difficulty of bringing such heavy guns into action, he bethought him whether equal range might not be obtained with lighter guns. He saw that if rifling was effective in small arms, it could not fail to be equally so in cannon. He saw that if wrought iron were employed instead of cast iron in the manufacture of ordnance, a great reduction of weight would be effected.

In December, 1854, he submitted to the Duke of Newcastle, Minister for War, a design showing the expediency of enlarging the ordinary rifle to the size of cannon, using elongated projectiles instead of cast iron balls. The idea so struck the Duke that he ordered six guns from Mr. Armstrong, to be made from that design.

The general principles of the gun were so simple that they recommended themselves to all, but the details were difficult to arrange. Armstrong knew, from the conservative feelings that always govern the War Office, that his invention would be looked upon with a supercilious eye. Subsequent events justified this opinion. It was important to deliver the first gun in a perfect state of efficiency. To do this he took a steel barrel capable of holding a 3-lb. shot, and wrapped around it a long bar of red-hot wrought iron; he then welded it into a solid cylinder. He next surrounded this by a second one, and welded it again, that again by a third one, and so on until the necessary thickness was built up. In this way he combined the maximum of strength with the minimum of weight.

The next thing was to practise with the gun and note its shooting powers. To do this he used to take it up into the wilds of Wearhead, among the lead mines and sheep farmers. There he would test it at all kinds of unseasonable hours. When the shepherd was wending his way at daybreak across the bleak moors, he would be startled by the report of cannon in his immediate vicinity. When the old dames were retiring at sunset, they would be alarmed by the sound of warfare on the generally peaceful hills. Many strange rumours were brought to Newcastle about the French having invaded the country, and marched up into the wilds of Durham at night-time.

It became necessary to remove his practising to other parts. The great difficulty was to find a place where there would be no danger, and where the secrets of his inventions would not be discovered by his competitors. The sands on the seashore formed his next practising ground, and at three o'clock he would be loading up and firing his little cannon, until the early bathers disturbed his work; then he would slip away, more like a culprit than a great inventor.

For three years he kept it from the Government. Nothing but indomitable perseverance sustained him through all the failures of imperfect guns and imperfect shells. At last the little 3-lb. cannon was completed, after a cost of thousands of pounds and three years of almost constant effort. It was delivered to the Government, and the colonels pronounced it a "pop-gun." But the gun and its inventor were too important facts to be sneered out of existence.

In 1858 General Peel appointed a committee to investigate the claims of rifled ordnance. In their report on Armstrong's "pop-gun" they say that there is nothing in the "Arabian Nights" half so wonderful as this new gun. The commander-in-chief said "it could do anything but speak."

A very large order was given to Armstrong for his new guns up to 32-pounders. The order was so large that the Elswick Works were enlarged to an enormous extent, and from that date Armstrong has been one of the wealthiest men in England.

When the transcendental importance of the great discovery was proved beyond a doubt, and the value of the patents was almost incalculable, Mr. Armstrong assigned all his interest in them as a free gift to the nation. He refused all remuneration from the Government. It paid him to do this. In return for his liberality he received the honour of knighthood and was made a Commander of the Bath, and it was found necessary to retain his services as engineer at the royal gun factory.

No man has done more to sustain British supremacy and to extend British possessions than Sir William Armstrong. The greatest general is dependent on the newest firearm, and this our hero has supplied.

WARREN HASTINGS.

A CENTURY and a-half ago, a boy of seven was playing by the side of a stream that ran through the lands of the lordly mansion of Daylesford, in Somersetshire. He was ill-fed, ill-clothed, and ignorant. His father had deserted him, his mother was dead, and his guardian was a bankrupt. But the stories that the poor ploughmen, with whose children he associated, loved to pour into his willing ears, of the former grandeur of his ancestors, had so filled his mind with a possible future, that the boy determined to try and buy back the mansion which his great-grandfather had lost. In his boyish enthusiasm, as he sat and gazed on all the lost grandeur, there arose in his mind a scheme which, through all the turns of his eventful career, was never abandoned. He would recover the estate which had belonged to his fathers. He would be Hastings of Daylesford. This purpose, formed in infancy and poverty, grew stronger as his intellect expanded, and as his fortune rose. When, under a tropical sun, he ruled fifty millions of people, his hopes, amid all the cares of war, finance, and legislation, still pointed to Daylesford.

There was nothing in Warren Hastings' youth that foretold the proud eminence which he achieved. In telling the method of success that he adopted, we shall have to gaze upon rivers of blood which he shed to accomplish his boyish hopes. We shall be compelled to listen to wailings from crushed hearts and hear cries from starving millions :—all that he may reach the position of his forefathers. The cheeks of a nation have blushed when the wrongs that were done by Warren Hastings on the poor Asiatics have been told.

He had a purpose in life, and he followed it. It led him to commit every crime of which the human mind is capable. The only satisfaction he received was the knowledge that he achieved what he set out to perform.

At seventeen years of age he went out to Calcutta as a clerk in the India Company's employ. He was placed at a desk in the secretary's office, and worked there two years. His attention to business caused the secretary to promote him to manage a branch office on the Hooghly. Though only nineteen years of age, he had the responsibility of representing the most wealthy Company in the world.

While he was thus employed the Nabob ruler declared war against England, took Hastings a prisoner, and incarcerated him with felons. He then marched on Calcutta, the governor fled, the town was taken, and most of the English perished in the Black Hole.

In these events originated the rise of Warren Hastings. The fugitive English governor had taken refuge on the dreary islet of Fulda. He was anxious to get information of the doings of the Nabob. No one seemed more likely than the young Englishman, who was made a prisoner at large in the immediate neighbourhood of the Nabob's Court. Hastings thus became a diplomatic agent, and soon established a high character for ability and resolution.

A conspiracy was being hatched by the Nabob and his counsellors to destroy all the English residents, and rid India of every European. Hastings, although quite alone among the conspirators, so managed matters as to be taken into the deliberations of the plotters. But the time for striking had not arrived, and Hastings, who was in extreme peril, fled to Fulda.

Soon after his arrival a body of British soldiers, commanded by Clive, came to the relief of the English governor. War was carried on against the Nabob, and Hastings volunteered as a soldier. During the early operations of the war he carried a musket. But the quick eye of Clive soon perceived that the head of the young volunteer would be more useful than his arm.   After the Battle of Plassey he was appointed to reside at the Court of the new prince as agent for the Company.

Six years after, when only about twenty-seven years of age, he was appointed a Member of Council, and was consequently forced to reside at Calcutta.   At this time Mr. Vansittart was governor of Bengal.   The business of a servant of the Company was simply to wring out of the natives one or two hundred thousand pounds as speedily as possible, that he might return home before his constitution was ruined by the heat, to marry a peer's daughter, and buy a rotten borough in Cornwall.

In eight years he had saved a comfortable fortune.   It was sufficient to retire upon, and he returned to England after investing his money in Calcutta at a usurious rate of interest.   High usury and bad security generally go together; and Hastings lost both interest and principal.   He soon began to look again towards India.   His pecuniary embarrassments drove him to accept another position as Member of Council at Madras.   His poverty was so extreme at this time that he had to borrow his passage-money to get out to his destination.

But he determined to make a bigger fortune this time, and to make it quickly—honestly if he could, but to make it.   No feelings of justice, morality, or kindness should stand in the way of his accomplishing his object.

At Madras he found the trade of the Company in a very dis-organised state.   The clerks were all turned warriors and nego-tiators, and instead of studying the interests of their employers they were lining their own pockets and robbing the poor Hindoos.   Hastings determined to remedy this state of things.   He thought if anyone was to have the privilege of impoverishing the natives for his own behoof, it should be the Company's governor, not the rank and file of commercial clerks.   In a few months he effected an important reform.   The directors notified to him their high appro-bation, and were so much pleased that they determined to place him at the head of the Government of Bengal.   Early in 1772 he went to Calcutta as governor.

Now his opportunities for piling up the money were unlimited.   A nation of fifty millions were prostrate at the feet of the ere-while book-keeper.   His first act was to take from the Nabob of Bengal one half his income: that is, one hundred and sixty thousand pounds.   His next feat of robbery was to steal from the Great Mogul his allowance of three hundred thousand pounds a-year, and, to add insult to robbery, he sent troops to seize two provinces of his domains.   These two provinces he sold to the Government of Oude for about half-a-million sterling.

These crimes were perpetrated in the name of the Company,

though he was strictly enjoined over and over again to do nothing that was not honest and fair.

But there was another matter to be settled by the Nabob and Hastings. The fate of a brave people was to be decided, and their wealth was to be seized.

Although he had stolen a mint of money, he was still greedy for more. The German baron who had sold his wife to Hastings was anxious for a settlement, and he soon departed with sufficient of the ill-gotten wealth to buy a large estate in Saxony.

The Rohillas were distinguished from the other inhabitants of India by courage in war and by skill in the arts of peace. While anarchy raged elsewhere, their little territory enjoyed the blessings of repose under the guardianship of valour. The Nabob of Bengal had set his heart on adding this district to his own. Right he had none. His own effeminate soldiers were useless to cope with such a people. He therefore approached Warren Hastings with the proposal to hire an English army with which to attack the inoffensive folk. He knew Hastings' greed for gold, and he knew his want of conscience when self-aggrandisement was offered.

A bargain was struck that an army should be lent to the Nabob, who should pay four hundred thousand pounds and all the expenses besides.

One brigade was sent under Colonel Champion to join the Nabob's forces and march against the Rohillas. They expostulated, entreated, offered a large ransom; but in vain. Hastings not merely sunk himself in the eyes of history, but he lowered England below the level of petty German baronies, who hired out their warriors for filthy lucre. But the lust for wealth was eating out the manhood from his heart, and the glamour of regaining Daylesford was too powerful to restrain him from crime. The threatened people resolved to defend themselves to the last. A bloody battle was fought. The desperate people gave proof of a superior military knowledge, and it is impossible to describe a more obstinate firmness of resolution than they displayed. The dastardly Nabob and his cowardly troupe of followers fled from the field. The English were left unsupported, but their fire and their charge were irresistible; after all the leaders of the Rohillas were slain the brave ranks gave way. Then the villainous ally of Hastings and his rabble made their appearance and plundered the camp of the valiant enemies whom they had never dared to look in the face. The British kept watch and guard whilst the pillaging proceeded.

Then the horrors of Indian war were let loose on the fair valleys of Rohilcund. The whole country was in a blaze. More than one hundred thousand people fled to the jungles, preferring famine and fever, and the haunts of the tiger, to the tyranny of him to whom an English and a Christian Government had, for shameful lucre, sold their substance and their blood, and the honour of their wives and daughters.

Remonstrations were sent to Hastings by his own officers, but he did not interfere, and he had made no conditions as to the mode in which the war was to be carried on. He had troubled himself about nothing except his four hundred thousand pounds. When the war ceased, the finest population in India was subjected to a greedy, cowardly, cruel tyrant. Commerce and agriculture languished. The rich province which had tempted the cupidity of the Nabob became the most miserable part even of his miserable domain.

Hastings, by these means, was not merely adding to his own fortunes, but he was adding to the dividends of the Company who employed him. No inquiries were made so long as the money was forthcoming, and the directors increased Hastings' salary as they magnified his power.

The wealth that he had accumulated enabled him to exercise great influence, not merely in India, but in England. Reports that had reached home of the crimes he was committing caused some inquiries by the Home Government; but his agents in London soon quieted all alarms, and laid the foundation for his stepping still higher in power and in wealth.

An Act was passed constituting him Governor-General of the whole of India for five years. Three Councillors were sent out to help him in administering affairs. He found the new Councillors were opposed to his style of robbery and deceit, and very soon a duel was fought between himself and a Mr. Francis.

The cause of this duel was alike disgraceful and contemptible to all concerned, both in its causes and its results. A wretched Hindoo, called Nuncomar, accused Hastings of putting offices up for sale, and of receiving bribes for suffering offenders to escape. He further alleged that a former native governor had been dismissed with impunity in consideration of a large sum paid to Hastings. The letter in which these allegations were made was handed to Mr. Francis, who read it aloud in the Council meeting. For doing this evident duty, he received a challenge from the haughty Governor-General, and was wounded in the shoulder.

The wretched Nuncomar was hunted to death by Hastings. He had the poor fellow thrown into gaol on a trumpery charge of forgery. Hastings' tool in the High Court of Calcutta tried him, condemned him, and pronounced sentence of death. The arrogance of the upstart governor would brook no hindrance to his hunt for wealth. Death was the consequence of standing in his way.

But the Home Government had been receiving further news of the rascally manner in which affairs were being managed. Hastings was removed from the position of Governor-General, and a Mr. Wheeler was sent out to supersede him. But these views

c

were not in accordance with those of Hastings. He refused to give up his position, and the state of affairs in the whole of the British Empire was such that he was able to defy the Government and to retain his seat.

More money was needed for himself, for his friends, and for the Company. Besides this, funds were needed to carry on a war with the French iu Southern India. His first design was on Benares, a city which in wealth, population, dignity, and sanctity was among the foremost of Asia. The Rajah of Benares was the first victim of Hastings' rapacity. He wanted a large supply of money. It was known that the Rajah had a large revenue, and it was suspected that he had a great treasure accumulated. The Rajah was suddenly called upon to pay a tribute of fifty thousand pounds; a few months elapsed, and he was called upon to pay the same sum again. After twelve months more the demand was renewed. The Rajah, in the hope of obtaining some indulgence, secretly offered Hastings a bribe of twenty thousand pounds. Hastings took the money. But danger of detection at last induced him to give it up. He paid over the bribe to the Company's treasury, and then turned round and compelled the poor Rajah to comply with his original demands, besides adding another ten thousand pounds as a further fine for bribing him. He sent troops to exact the money.

The money was paid. But this was not enough. Hastings determined to plunder the Rajah, and for that end he fastened a quarrel on him by requiring him to keep a large body of cavalry for the British service. He objected, and resisted. This was just what Hastings wanted.

A larger demand was now made, and was resisted. Then a larger still, with the like results. A much larger demand still was now imperiously called for, and the remonstrances of the poor Rajah were treated as a crime. He was punished by confiscating all his possessions. He had offered two hundred thousand pounds to propitiate his rapacious enemy. But half-a-million was demanded.

Before an answer could be returned Hastings marched on Benares, arrested the Rajah, and caused such a tumult in the sacred city that he nearly precipitated a rebellion that might have cost the British their possessions in India. Every soldier and all the officers who went with him lost their lives in his unrighteous cause, and he himself was nearly killed with his whole staff.

Our space is too limited to follow this adventurer through all his acts of "vaulting ambition." Suffice it that he laid up treasure of a vast amount that was soon stripped from him by the lawyers in London. His trial for impeachment lasted eight years. During all that time he was compelled to fee the most able lawyers in the land. He subsidised newspapers to espouse his cause. He had paid agents travelling through the country to advance his interests in different ways; and witnesses were brought in large numbers from long distances at an enormous expense.

After his trial was over he had barely enough left for consummating the object of his life. Daylesford was bought, and for twenty years the old man led a quiet life in the home of his forefathers, and was buried on the spot where eighty years before he had lain in childish fancies and dreamed of regaining his father's home.

SIR JOHN BROWN.

WHEN John Brown was apprenticed to a Sheffield firm no one seemed to see in his character the genius which he afterwards developed. He was emphatically a "Sheffield blade." His main cause of success was the fact that he always kept his eyes open to look for chances of making money.

He had not been apprenticed long before his employers found out that they possessed a youth of wonderful energy and indomitable perseverance. The apprentice very soon stepped to the front. As soon as his time was out he was offered a partnership by the senior member of the firm. But the small amount of capital that he was able to raise was not sufficient to enable him to enter the firm.

His business ability had so impressed Mr. Earl that he was determined to do something for the youth. He next offered to sell him the factoring branch of their trade, and volunteered to help him to raise the requisite funds. By a few of his friends guaranteeing £500 to a local bank he made a start in life. This insignificant capital soon began to grow, and when he sold out to a limited company a few years ago, it amounted to the princely sum of £1,000,000.

He remained in the cutlery trade for some years, and saved a little money with which to launch out into the manufacture of steel on his own account.

In 1848 he made the first step upwards in his successful career. He noticed the damage that was done to railway trucks by the want of a buffer between them. As the result of a long series of experiments he invented the conical spring buffer, and patented it.

The next great difficulty was to get the companies to adopt it. There was no doubt of the value of the invention, but while the railways were making up their minds to apply it, the inventor must wait. None of the English railways would entertain the

idea at first. The managers declared that they were satisfied with
their present arrangements, and they were in no mood to make
expensive alterations.

Brown knew that until the thing had been practically tested by
some railway he could never reap his reward. All the big lines
pooh-poohed the idea.

At last a small line in South Wales, called the Taff Vale
Railway, gave an order for a pair, as a test. This was soon
followed by a larger order, and the Glasgow line followed suit by
ordering a pair. The next order was from a small Irish railway.

By this time the value of the buffers was pretty well tested,
and the London & North-Western Railway sent an enormous
order. So large was this order that Brown was unable to fulfil it
in his works. He went and bought a much larger place, and set
to work to make the springs. He knew that his fortune was
made. Orders began to pour in upon him much faster than he
expected. He bought more buildings and engaged more men,
and still he could not keep pace with the demand. He bought
more land, and more buildings were erected, but his place was still
not large enough.

In 1864 an opportunity occurred of purchasing the Atlas Works.
At that time they only occupied about three acres of ground.
They now cover thirty acres.

The enormous amount of iron and steel that he was using was
nearly all brought from Sweden. It occurred to him that the
Yorkshire iron and the Yorkshire coal might be used to produce
all he wanted. He would thus save profit and carriage. No
sooner said than done. When his ironworks were started he found
that his neighbours wanted him to supply them, and it was soon
necessary to build more furnaces.

The original works were altogether too small to produce what
was needed to meet the demand. Ten converting furnaces were
built near the railway. This was the introduction of the iron
trade into Sheffield. Up to this date Sheffield had been merely a
cutlery town. John Brown was the father of the iron trade in
South Yorkshire. He was spoken of as one of the most successful
men in the town, but his great stroke of fortune was yet to be
made.

In the autumn of 1860 he was returning from a tour in Europe,
and came home *viâ* Toulon. The French man-of-war *La Gloire*
was at that time in the harbour. This was the ship that caused
such a consternation in our Admiralty offices. It was the first
timber-built ship that carried armour-plate four and a-half inches
thick. So great was the scare that our Admiralty stopped the
building of ten men-of-war that were to carry one hundred guns
each. They were stopped to be changed into armour-plated vessels
like the French ship.

The plates on *La Gloire* were five feet long and two feet wide, and were made by hammer—a most expensive and unreliable method of preparing them. But at that time there was no other method known.

Mr. Brown knew of the sensation that had been caused by the new invention, and determined to try and see for himself whether some improvement could not be effected that might bring wealth to his own pocket and glory to his country. He tried to get on board the ship, but his broad English face discovered his nationality, and he was not allowed. He spent some time in examining the outside thoroughly, and came to the conclusion that the armour-plates used in clothing her could be rolled.

His mind was made up. He felt convinced that he could roll a plate more uniform in quality than it could be hammered, besides being more tenacious. He hurried off home and set to work.

The first difficulty was to find any slotting machines sufficiently large to manipulate the immense masses he intended to roll. He could buy nothing strong enough. Mr. Shanks, the well-known machine maker of Glasgow, showed him his most powerful productions. Mr. Brown explained that they were not strong enough to do his work.

" You cannot break them," said Mr. Shanks.

" Yes, but you don't know what I want them for. Nothing that has been produced may break them, but I must have them stronger."

Having agreed for a certain price per ton, he called for the tracings, and taking a pencil he strengthened the parts where the strain would be most severe ; then handed the designs back. The new machines were nearly double the strength of any then produced.

Something like £10,000 was expended in experiments and machinery before satisfactory results were achieved. At length he found, after months of patient toil, that his invention was a grand success. He rolled out a sheet of iron five inches thick, three feet wide, and twenty feet long—an unparalleled feat. He knew now that millions would be his reward if he could only overcome the official repugnance to his new plan of making plates. The British admiralty wanted armour-plates, but they seemed to labour under the impression that nothing would answer except hammered iron !

Lord Palmerston was then Premier of England. Great changes were taking place in the ordnance of the different armies. The Armstrong rifled cannon were able to pierce any ships then built. Ordinary ironclads were smashed like frail rowboats. Krupp was making cannon at Antwerp that would destroy any navy. The minds of the Government grew anxious. This was Brown's opportunity. He invited Lord Palmerston to visit his works and see for himself the process of smelting, casting, heating, and rolling plates, six inches thick and eighteen or twenty feet long, weighing six tons.

Palmerston accepted the invitation, he satisfied himself that the process was superior to hammering, and as a result, large orders were given for the navy. So enormous were these orders that by 1863 Brown had clad in mail fully three-fourths of the whole British navy. The most of these were covered by four and a-half inch plates. The Government appeared to have come to the conclusion that nothing thicker was feasible.

Some trials were made with steel plates of that thickness, but the first shot smashed them in every instance. The iron plate of extra thickness made by Brown showed no damage until it had been hit by thirty-four shots. This was a splendid day for Brown and for Sheffield. His fame spread throughout the whole civilised world. The *Times* contained long articles on the wonderful progress of modern armaments.

Foreign nations were anxious to secure the services of Brown. Russia made overtures of a most lucrative nature, but he steadfastly adhered to his rule of never accepting any orders from a foreign government without the sanction of the home officials. During the American war he refused large orders from the Northern States on these grounds.

But the limit of his views was not yet reached. He saw that any ironclad of that date could be pierced by a shot from a rifled cannon. He was anxious to get the Government to clothe some ships in armour twenty inches thick. The Lords of the Navy were blank with astonishment. They pictured to themselves floating coffins for the Marines that would sink at the slightest provocation, if they ever floated at all. Practical men doubted the possibility of either rolling such plates or of putting them together when rolled.

"Much success had made the man mad," evidently. But in April, 1863, he enlarged his works for the purpose of putting into operation his scheme for rolling plates that would weigh nearly fifteen tons. In April the Lords of the Admiralty, headed by the Duke of Somerset, visited the new works to see the latest invention. They saw that their host was true to his promise, for he rolled plates with every success, much thicker than had ever been dreamt of before.

Now came the difficulty of realising from his success. He had spent something like one hundred thousand pounds in his discoveries, and no plate that he had made would resist the latest pattern of ordnance turned out by Armstrong. The nation cried a halt. If it were to be a neck-and-neck race between cannon and armour, let the inventors spend their own money in the fun. Millions were as good as wasted already, of the nation's money, in the useless ships already constructed.

John Brown was now sufficiently great to be listened to by the folk in authority. He wrote to the Government what sounds very much like a challenge. He offered to make some armour that he asserted no shots could penetrate. The letter stipulated for a certain description of target, and agreed also that if the plates did not resist the largest ordnance of the day, he should receive no pay for his experimental plates. The challenge was accepted. The plates were made, and resisted every shot that was fired at them.

After this the Atlas Works made rapid progress. In a short time they were known all over the world. The plates prepared for the Italian ironclad, *The Duilio*, are twenty-two inches thick.

The first year of Brown's business was represented by £3,000. The last year it amounted to a million.

To him, more than to any other man, is due the revolution which has taken place in the navies of the world. His patriotism caused him to offer all his productions to his own country, and England to-day owes more to John Brown, for her supremacy on the seas, than she gives him credit for. In 1867 the honour of knighthood was conferred as an acknowledgment of his services.

SIR WILLIAM FAIRBAIRN.

ONE of the first glimpses we get of our hero's life is in the Highlands of Scotland. When about ten years of age his life's duty consisted of nursing his younger brother Peter, a delicate child, two years of age. To relieve himself of the labour of carrying him about, he began the construction of a little waggon in which to wheel him. All the tools he possessed were a gimlet, a table knife, and an old saw. With these and a piece of thin board and a few nails, he managed to make a waggon body. The chief difficulty was in making the wheels. He contrived to surmount this by sawing four slices off a stem of a tree, and boring holes through the centre with a red-hot poker. The little waggon was then put on the four wheels, and to the delight of its maker was found to answer well. In this carriage he wheeled the future Sir Peter Fairbairn, mayor of Leeds.

Here was the foundation of the future fortune. The ingenious little mechanic, with the hot poker, the knife, and saw, became the future builder of the first iron ships. He revolutionised the mercantile navies of the world.

The next view we get of Fairbairn is at a colliery near North Shields. He was then only fifteen years of age. His Scotch accent marked him out among the pit lads, and he was the object

of much annoyance at their hands.   The chief pastime amongst
these youths was boxing, and Fairbairn had to run the gauntlet of
the whole district before he could get any peace.   A happy
thought occurred to him.   There was one of the lads who was
recognised as the champion boxer of the pit, and he determined to
have a round with him.   If he was victor he would be respected
and get some peace.   If he lost the fight he would leave the place,
and start anew at some other colliery.   He was loth to leave, as
his position was improving.   He had already fought fifteen pitched
battles, and was the winner in most of them.   But the insults to
which he was almost a daily martyr brought him several times to
the point of abandoning the work altogether.

The whole neighbourhood came to see the fight.   Even the
women were anxious that the Tyneside lad should beat the young
Scotchman.   The pits for miles around were represented at the
struggle.   It was a protracted affair, and at one time Fairbairn
felt as though he must give in.   But the recollection of what
victory meant for him nerved him to make another effort.   He stood
firmly waiting the last crushing onslaught of his opponent.   The
hundreds of spectators were excitedly cheering on the lads, and he
knew his only chance was to keep cool.   His strength was almost
exhausted, so was his antagonist's.   The one who remained calm
would come off victor.   There was more hanging in the balance
in this struggle than the spectators realised; for had the fight
gone against the Scotch lad, the flow of national events might
have been changed.   If that sturdy little boy from Kelso gets
beaten, he will leave his situation, and the future millionaire might
be only a struggling labourer for life.   But the onslaught was met
by a well-defended effort, which so surprised the other lad that he
was off his guard for an instant.   That instant was the opportunity
that Fairbairn grasped.   He assumed the offensive, and so eagerly
followed it up that soon the Tynesider was prostrate on the
ground.   There were no more persecutions for young Fairbairn
after that.   He rose at one bound to the topmost notch in the
estimation of his mates, and this had its effects on his own
character, besides helping to raise him in the eyes of his superiors.

He soon was received into the office of the owners as an articled
engineer.   His wages were not large, but by working overtime he
was able to add much to them, and thus assist his father's family,
who were struggling with small means and large expenses.

Besides working overtime he studied.   His programme was as
follows : Monday, arithmetic ; Tuesday, history ; Wednesday,
novels ; Thursday, algebra ; Friday, euclid ; and Saturday,
poetry.

When he had finished his apprenticeship he made up his mind to
go out into the world in search of experience.   Work being scarce
on the Tyne he determined to try London.   He took passage by a

Shields coal ship as being the cheapest route. The crew consisted of a few old men and two or three boys. The captain was generally drunk, and as the weather proved rough, Fairbairn and his friend had to work to help to manage the ship. They arrived in London after a tedious voyage of fourteen days, minus several spars and an anchor.

His experience in London was described by himself, at a meeting in Derby, as follows: "When I first entered London, a young man from the country had no chance whatever of success, in consequence of the trade guilds and unions. I had no difficulty in finding employment, but before I could begin work I had to run the gauntlet of the trade societies, and after dancing attendance for nearly six weeks with very little money in my pocket, and having to 'box Harry' all the time, I was ultimately declared illegitimate, and sent adrift to seek my fortune elsewhere."

His first attempt to work in London having thus disastrously ended, the two youths determined to try their fortune in the country. They started before daylight one morning with a few coppers in their pockets. The roads were covered with slush and snow. The youthful adventurers had no settled plan. After eight hours of steady walking in a northerly direction, during which they only indulged in a penny roll and some ale, they came to Hertford. They were wet to the skin and shivering with cold, but they at once sought for work at a millwright's shop. He could give them no work, but seeing their sorry plight offered Fairbairn half-a-crown. His spirit revolted at the idea of taking money he had not earned. He declined with thanks, and turned from the door to seek elsewhere. The two, wet, weary, hungry, and disheartened, went into the churchyard for a rest. They sat down on a tombstone to talk over matters, the companion relieving himself by a good cry, and an occasional outburst of "Why didn't you take the half-crown?"

"Come, cheer up," said Fairbairn. "It's no use crying, let's try another road."

They started off again, but at the first bridge the disheartened youth broke down again.

"I willna' gang a bit further, let's go back to London."

Fairbairn again cheered him up, and they got lodgings for the night in a common lodging-house.

Next day they walked seven miles without breakfast, and got work on a windmill. After saving £3, our hero returned to London and got work at a ropery. While here he still spent all his spare time in studying. He made up his mind that there was plenty of room in the engineering business for inventive minds. In a conversation with Mr. Rennie, the great engineer, he asked him if he thought there was room in the business.

" Ay, my lad," said Rennie, "there's plenty of room in the top storeys, the lower rooms are always full." Fairbairn never forgot this. It was said half in irony, but it had a splendid effect. He got to the top storey.

The first model that he made on his own account was a success in the working, but he never got paid for it. The second was a sausage machine, which he not only invented but also constructed. This was his first decided success.

But when work again became scarce in London, he started on foot for South Wales to gain further experience. He walked through Bath, Bristol, Newport, and Cardiff without finding work. He then took ship for Dublin, and landed with three-halfpence in his pocket. The second day he got employment at making some patterns for the nail-making machines, then recently introduced. His employer was fast losing his trade through the English competitors making their nails by machinery. He wanted to give Ireland the benefit of the manufacture.

Making this machinery occupied Fairbairn all the summer. When finished Mr. Robinson dare not use it, as the workmen threatened to strike if it were put to use. The nail trade soon left Dublin, and has never been revived. Such a town as this was of no use to the young engineer. He left for Liverpool, and proceeded to Manchester, where he settled down and married. He had little money and few friends, but he soon made both.

After working for two years as a millwright at good wages, he started for himself with the small amount he had saved. He and a shopmate named Lillie formed a partnership, and hired a small shed at twelve shillings a-week. These two working men with corduroy clothes, in a paltry little shed, seemed of no moment to Manchester or its people, but, before many years were past, not merely Manchester, but the whole world heard of them. It was a good thing for Manchester that the two grimy-faced men, with their trumpery shed and their insignificant capital, started there.

Their first job was a loss, as it turned out to be an infraction of some one's patent. They next set to work and made a powerful lathe, which was capable of turning shafts six inches in diameter. With this they obtained a few orders, but barely sufficient to keep them going. At last Lillie determined to give up the partnership, and return to weekly wages. Fairbairn saw that it would never do to succumb at such a time. He argued with his partner, but to little avail. As a last resource he suggested that they should get some business cards printed and become their own travellers by calling upon the various manufacturers.

In their best Sunday clothes, and with their business-looking cards, "Fairbairn & Lillie," they made a tour of the principal firms. Amongst others Fairbairn called on Murrays, the large cotton spinners. He was favourably received, and told to call next day with his partner.

That was a heart-beating time for Fairbairn. His whole future depended on this first piece of work. Mr. Murray must have been favourably impressed with this interview. Next day, when the two called, he took them over his mill and inquired if they were in a position to renew the whole of the shafts in the factory.

This was far more than they had ever dreamt of. It almost took away their breath. They had no adequate plant to undertake such a contract. They had no capital, no workshop, and no credit. But they had plenty of confidence in themselves, and they did not propose to let such a chance slip by. They boldly replied that they were willing and well able to execute the work.

Mr. Murray said he would call and see them at their own workshop to satisfy himself. Here their hearts sank into their boots. The prize that was just within their reach disappeared as they were about to grasp it. When Murray saw the " nakedness of the land," and realised what a tumble-down concern the firm and its shed was, he would go no further in the business.

Next morning he paid his promised visit. He saw the wooden shed, the sturdy Irishman who turned the lathe standing idly waiting for work, and the two partners. It was the individual merit of the men that covered the multitude of shortcomings. He gave them the order, and they started to work with light hearts. They worked from five in the morning to nine at night for a long time, and finished the alterations within the required time. Every part of the work was carefully done, and to Mr. Murray's entire satisfaction.

This was their first work at any cotton machinery. It enabled them to study a new class of work, and while doing so Fairbairn noticed that there was room for immense improvement. He mentioned his views to a millowner, who only rewarded him by a sneer. However, he and his partner made up their minds to try. The result was that they revolutionised one part of the engineering trade. Up to this time the couplings of the different driving shafts had been so badly arranged in all factories that scarcely a week passed without a breakdown, stopping the whole mill and necessitating Sunday work for repairs. After Fairbairn's improvements were introduced, Sunday work for engineers was almost abolished.

The completion of Murray's order gave a great impetus to their business. He recommended them to his friends, and among others to the largest firm of cotton spinners in the kingdom. McConnel & Kennedy engaged Fairbairn to put in all the machinery in their new factory; a contract that required the united energy and all the time of both partners. A larger shop was rented and more hands employed, and soon the little world around Manchester was talking of the two rising mechanics.

Everything was done so well, and the men were so steady and hard-working, that they got abundance of credit, and began to creep up in the business world.

Fairbairn at this time was designer, draughtsman, and book-keeper. He rose at four or five, and often worked till ten at night. At the end of five years they were worth £5,000, which was all sunk in machinery and tools. Borrowing some money from Heywood's bank, they bought a second-hand boiler and engine, and leased some ground for building upon. Orders were now plentiful enough. They soon got more work than they could finish. They had more orders than capital. But the name of Fairbairn was in the front rank of engineering millwrights.

Our space will not allow us to follow this hero through all his successes. We should like to tell of the wonderful water-wheels which he built, and which are now acknowledged to be the most perfect ever constructed. We should like to tell our readers of his successes in building the first iron ships, and of his difficulty in the management of the compass while affected by the proximity of iron.

Such ingenuity, such perseverance, and such wonderful steadiness were bound to be paid by grand results. Fairbairn not merely made a name that is honoured throughout the world, but he secured for himself an honourable wealth and a title that he long lived to enjoy.

PETER COOPER,
Of New York.

On a summer's day, in 1796, in a narrow lane in New York, five boys were engaged in scraping the dry, brown mortar from between the bricks of the walls. The dust they called snuff. They collected it in tin mugs, and with it they intended to play at shopkeeping. Suddenly an ugly-looking dog sprang out upon them, and in a moment four of the embryo merchants had disappeared. Only one remained, and he, the smallest and weakest, stood firmly to his ground. He held tightly to his cup of sham snuff, and with an instinct which was to bring him fame and fortune in the future, turned about and faced the danger. The dog seemed cowed by the bravery of the little fellow, and went back to the house from which it had so suddenly emerged, and the child, still guarding his treasure in the cup, walked after his companions. This little hero was Peter Cooper.

The incident was the earliest recollection of the man who ran the first locomotive over the Ohio Railway; who helped to lay the Atlantic cable; who gave to America her noblest institute, and

who earned and gave away millions of dollars. At seventeen he
was apprenticed to a coach-builder, and spent most of his spare
time in study. While the other apprentices were engaged in
dancing with loose characters, in witnessing cock-fights, or
drinking, he retired to his little room, and, braving the jeers of
his companions, devoted his evenings to coach-panel carving, and
other light work, from which he realised a fair profit. When he
was twenty-one, and out of his apprenticeship, he went to his
employer to bid him good-bye. A surprise was in store for him.
Instead of bidding him good-bye, the employer, who had been a
silent witness of all his doings, said :

"Peter, you have done good work for me. I will build you a
shop and set you up in business for yourself ; you may pay me
when you can."

The offer was a tempting one, but, with many thanks, the
young man declined it. He had no capital, and had made up his
mind that he would not commence life by burdening himself with
debt. He never regretted this action.

He started out to seek his fortune, knowing that he must depend
upon his own exertions for success. After working for three
years at six shillings a-day, he had saved enough to buy the right
of making a patent cloth-shearing machine for the whole of the
State of New York. The business proved a successful one. In a
short while he was in possession of £100, a sum that he then
regarded as a fortune. He was quite elated with his success, and
contemplated launching out into a larger way of business. But
he happened to visit his parents previous to starting afresh, and
found his aged father swamped with debts which he was unable
to pay. The sheriff was on the point of selling him out of house
and home. Young Cooper at once paid out the whole of his little
fortune in redeeming the family from ruin. He had to start in
the world afresh, without any capital, and burdened with some of
his father's debts, which he guaranteed to meet as they matured.
He now had a wife to keep, and the probability of supporting his
parents for the rest of their lives.

Like a brave young fellow that he was, he buckled to and set
to work to make more money. He afterwards declared that his
necessities at this time were the making of him. His faculties
were sharpened by his needs, and he soon developed such improvements in his cloth-shearing machine that he was able to patent
them. It now became the most desirable one in the market, and
as the war with England stopped the import of all English cloths,
a very large profit was made in the business.

He made hay while the sun shone. At the close of the war the
demand for his machines fell off and he left the business, but he
had enough saved to buy a lot of land in the city of New York,
on which he built some houses and a glue factory. This was no

sooner developed into a success than he began the manufacture of oil, and after conducting that to a successful issue he started to make whiting, chalk, and isinglass. Everything prospered with him. The difficulties of his younger days had sharpened his wits, and he soon was recognised as one of the smartest business men in the city.

His credit increased with his business. No payment ever matured without being met. He lived to be ninety-three years of age, and he often boasted that no debt of his ever fell due without being paid. He might with equal truth have said that no business he ever undertook failed. Many a time his grandest enterprises were nearly crushed by unforeseen circumstances, but his ready resources never failed to recover them.

In 1828 he bought, partly on credit, three thousand acres of land within the city limits of Baltimore, costing about one hundred thousand dollars. This was bought in partnership with two other men, who promised to meet their share of the payments as they fell due. But he soon found that their wealth was all imaginary, and he had to shoulder the whole of the debt himself. In this piece of land he secured all the shore line of Baltimore for three miles in one direction. It was a splendid chance if he could only develop the property and meet the payments.

There was great excitement at this time about the prospect of a railway being opened from Baltimore to Ohio. The line was nearly finished, but capital was wanting to complete it. The shareholders were unwilling to subscribe any more capital. They doubted the ability to run an engine round some of the curves and over some of the gradients. One of the finest railways in the world was in danger of being abandoned.

Mr. Cooper knew that if this line was not finished his immense tract of land would be a losing speculation. All his capital would be sunk in a valueless property, and the difference between being a millionaire and a pauper hinged on the completion of this railway. His remonstrances were to no purpose ; the shareholders would not subscribe another cent. They would rather lose what money they had already invested than throw more good money after bad.

But Cooper knew that this line must be finished or he would be a bankrupt. He set to work with all his energy and had an engine constructed after his own pattern, specially adapted for rounding sharp curves and climbing steep grades. He put it on the track and fastened to it a corn truck. With the utmost difficulty he persuaded a number of the shareholders to meet together and see the ease with which all the difficulties would be overcome.

The most eminent engineer of the district had reported that no train could be run on such a line. The citizens believed this, and looked upon Cooper's attempts as the whim of a land speculator who simply wanted to sell out his tract to get rid of a bad bargain. But about a couple of hundred shareholders assembled, and Mr. Cooper put thirty or forty of them into the truck and started his engine.

As the strange-looking train went slowly out, the half-concealed contempt of the crowd was manifested by certain remarks about " widows" and " coffins " being more numerous in a short time. The engine went steadily along and more steam was applied, and the faster it went the steadier it moved.   A gradient of twenty feet to the mile had to be overcome, and no one but Cooper and the engine-driver thought it could climb it.   More steam was put on, and the eager faces of the nervous passengers looked doubtfully as the worst part was approached.   They naturally thought their lives and their fortunes depended on this trip.   If Cooper was right, the future for each of them was brighter, and the history of Baltimore was changed.

Twenty miles an hour was made, and the great railroad was saved from bankruptcy and abandonment.   The new shares were clamoured for, and the old shares sold at a premium.

It was now feasible to do something with the three thousand acres.   Large iron works were built, and ironstone was dug from the land. Wood was cut off part of the land to make into charcoal for manufacturing charcoal-iron.   Lots of money was invested in this way, but it did not pay very well.   There was too much capital sunk in land and buildings.   Interest and wages were too high, and prices were cut down by English competition.

In his efforts to make it pay Mr. Cooper constructed some novel kilns for burning charcoal that nearly cost him his life.   They were circular in form, hooped round with iron at the top, and arched over.   The idea was to make them nearly air-tight, with single bricks left out that the fire might be smothered when the wood was sufficiently burned.   On one occasion, when the kiln was half emptied the coal itself took fire, and the workmen attempted in vain to put it out with water.   They at last gave it up in despair.   Then Mr. Cooper himself went to the door, and had hardly reached it, when the gas, generated by the coal, exploding, enveloped him in flames, and hurled him several feet in the air.   His eyebrows, hair, and whiskers were burnt off, and he barely escaped with his life.   His eyes were so injured that he had to remain in a darkened room for five months.

Mr. Cooper determined to sell his Baltimore property to a large Boston Company, and take most of the payment in shares. He knew that if there was capital enough to thoroughly develop it, it would pay splendidly.   He sold out for about the same amount as he paid, and took the hundred dollar shares at forty-five dollars a share.   This was the " lucky" turn in the history of the future millionaire.   The shares began to rise in value, soon the forty-five dollar shares were worth one hundred and fifty. They crept up gradually until they reached two hundred and thirty dollars. Then Mr. Cooper sold out, and was counted among the millionaires of the world.

When he returned to New York with his wealth, the honour of being elected an alderman was offered him by his old neighbours. A committee was appointed to wait upon him with this view.

"But I have my business to attend to; I don't want to be an alderman."

"But you must be," said the solemn chairman of the committee.

"But I won't be," replied Mr. Cooper, and the deputation retired.

Next day a larger deputation waited upon him to urge the nomination.

"I'll tell you what I'll do," he said, "I'll give you five thousand dollars towards the election fund, if you'll let me off." The offer was refused. He was elected, and did more to redeem his native city than any other man.

With his great wealth he started some large iron works at Trenton, and his success continued. His capital increased beyond all expectation. He determined to find some suitable way of investing a part of his money so that it would benefit mankind. A friend of his who had visited Paris spoke to him of the free education there afforded to thousands of poor young men. This was the germ that ripened into the magnificent institute, which cost a million dollars, that was presented to the American nation. The Cooper Institute is for the board and education (free) of any suitable young persons, whose only claim is their willingness to learn and their inability to pay.

In the rapid whirl of English and American life it is not to be wondered at that the origin of great enterprises should be soon forgotten. The peoples of the world have become so familiar with the use of telegraph cables that they are apt to forget the men who first found the means, and who stood the brunt of the battle while others were coldly standing by to scoff at their efforts.

In the year 1854, five gentlemen met in New York to form the New York, Newfoundland, and London Telegraph Company. Peter Cooper was made president of that company, and to him, as much as to any single man, is due the successful completion of the Atlantic cable. The first deep-sea cable was laid under his supervision. At Port Basque he went on board the vessel chartered to carry the cable, and, with flags flying and the crews cheering, the ship weighed anchor and was ready to be taken in tow by the steamer. At the outset there was an accident, caused by the

captain of the tug.   In the effort to make her fast by the cable, he
came into violent collision, tore away her quarter-rail and shrouds,
and at last carried the vessel out of the harbour with such force
that the cable broke.   After a delay of several hours in splicing it,
he was signalled to come round and once more take the cable-ship
in tow.   In doing this he managed to get the towing-line entangled
in the wheel of the steamer, and at last was obliged to cut it.   He
did this so awkwardly that the line swung round the anchor of
the cable-ship, and the anchor was lost.

The position of Mr. Cooper and his friends was now most
perilous.   Their vesssel was without an anchor.   A storm sprang
up.   The ship began to drift rapidly toward a reef of rocks, upon
which it seemed for a time as if she must be dashed to pieces.   At
last, however, the steamer came up, the line was made fast, and
the trip to sea commenced.   But it was not successful.   Owing to
the blunders of the captain of the steamer, the wire had to be cut
and eventually was dropped into the sea, causing a loss to the
company of 300,000 dollars.

In two years, Mr. Cooper's company had another cable ready.
It was successfully laid to Newfoundland, and the first link in the
chain of telegraphic communication with Europe was finished.
Following up this beginning, Mr. Cooper and his friends determined to lay a cable across the Atlantic.   For this purpose they
dispatched Mr Cyrus W. Field to London to obtain subscriptions.
His appeals were successful.   The 3,000 miles of wire were contracted for, and put on two vessels that were to meet in mid-ocean.
The scheme was universally laughed at,and Mr.Cooper was regarded
as a millionaire lunatic, whose wealth had driven him demented.
But the project went on, the cable was completed, the ships met
in mid-ocean, the ends of the wire were united, and the whole
world was startled by the announcement that the Queen had sent
a message to the President.   New York and London were wild
with excitement.   Even the ponderous *Times* seemed juvenile with
joy.   The dream of enthusiasts was at last a realised fact.

There was much rejoicing among Mr. Cooper's associates.   But
their joy was short-lived.   After about five hundred messages had
been received the cable ceased to work, and the sneers of the
people who remark " I told you so !" were pretty frequent.   Many
men loudly declared that no messages had ever been received
through it.   Fortunately the English Government had transmitted
messages that were of vital importance while conducting their war
with China.   Therefore, no doubt existed as to its practicability,
and no trouble was experienced in launching another company to
put down another cable.   The cable was made and laid half-way
across the ocean, and then lost.

The company was now on the verge of financial ruin.   Mr.
Field was again sent by Mr. Cooper to England to raise more

D

money. At first people laughed at him, but he was instructed not
to return until the money was subscribed, and he at last succeeded.
The third cable was successfully laid and worked to perfection.

The lost half of the second wire was now grappled for, and, to
the bewilderment of the whole world, was at last fished out of the
depths of the ocean. It was joined to the other half, and two
cables were connecting the two continents. This feat was performed in a depth of water two and a-half miles deep, and is said
to be unparalleled in the history of the world. It was pulled up
three times before it was secured. They got it up just far enough
to see it, but it dropped down again, and they had to do the work
over again.

This lifted the company out of the slough of despond and placed
it on the highest pinnacle of success. The shares ran up in value
to a fabulous height, and Mr. Cooper was now " rolling in wealth."

He was afterwards nominated for President of the United
States, but was not elected. He lived to the age of ninety-three,
and went down to his rest respected by the whole nation.

THE MARQUIS OF NORMANBY.

THE lordly owners of Mulgrave Castle in Yorkshire must trace
their wealth and their position back to a certain Yankee ship's
carpenter named Phipps.

At a little town called Woolich, in the State of Maine, a gun-
smith's wife bore twenty-six children. One of these was William
Phipps, the founder of the present house of Mulgrave. The quiet
life of a shepherd did not suit the lad. He longed to be a sailor,
and seek adventures through the world. But not being able to
find a ship that would take him, he apprenticed himself to a shipbuilder. He learned to read and write during his leisure hours.

One of his methods of success was not in any way noted for its
originality, although it was a success so far as it went. After
finishing his apprenticeship he wooed and married a wealthy
widow, and with her money set up as a shipbuilder. For ten
years he carried this on, and gradually increased his wealth. But
his adventurous spirit seemed to revolt at the patient plodding
necessary for a shipbuilder. He wanted to make money fast.

His opportunity came thus: As he was standing in the streets
of Boston he overheard some sailors speaking of a wreck that had
taken place somewhere in the West Indies. It was a Spanish ship,
and was supposed to have money on board. Selling off his
business and choosing a crew of likely men, he set sail for the
Bahamas.

He had no difficulty in finding the wreck, and as it was close inshore he soon recovered the cargo. But the money was not to be found. The result was that he only made a trifle by the expedition.

His success, however, was sufficient to whet his appetite for a further trial, and when he heard of another wreck he determined to try again. This one was far more richly laden, in fact the cargo was mainly silver bars and golden coins. The wreck had occurred half-a-century before, and there was some doubt as to its exact position, but he forthwith formed the resolution of trying to raise the wreck, or trying to fish up the treasure.

He was not rich enough to undertake the adventure single-handed, so he sailed for England to try and get powerful help. His fame in raising the wreck off the Bahamas had preceded him. He applied direct to the Government. His enthusiasm succeeded in overcoming the slowness of the officials. Charles II. placed at his disposal a ship of about twenty guns, and manned with one hundred sailors. He was appointed commander of the expedition.

Phipps then set sail for Port de la Plata, to find the Spanish wreck and try to bring up the buried wealth. The wreck had occurred fifty years before, and he had nothing but the rumours of tradition to guide him in his search. There was a long coast to explore, and a wide stretch of sea, without any trace of the golden argosy that lay silently buried below.

Phipps was a man of dogged perseverance and unflagging hope. He set his men to drag along the coast for weeks together. But nothing rewarded their efforts except sea-weed, bits of rock and shell-fish. Still he kept them at work. They grumbled at the monotony of the occupation, but he still kept them to dragging. Of all occupations in the world this was the most unsuited to sailors. Their complaints grew louder, and as the work proceeded, with no satisfactory results, they began to think that the commander was a madman, who had led them on a fool's errand.

At last the most restless spirits began to gain headway. One day the men broke into open mutiny. Several of them in a body marched on to the quarter-deck, and demanded that the voyage should be relinquished. But the mutineers had miscalculated the temper of the man with whom they had to deal. No intimidation would deter him. He seized the ringleaders, and sent the others back to their duty.

The ship needed some repairs, and to do this it was necessary to bring her close up to a small island, and lighten her by taking out the stores. The spirit of discontent still showed itself among the crew. A new plot was made to seize the ship, throw Phipps into the sea, and start on a cruise of plundering in the South Seas. The whole plan was formed, and everything was ripe for putting it into execution, when it was discovered that the assistance of the ship's carpenter would be requisite to a successful carrying out of the plot. He was made privy to the designs and asked to join. He proved faithful to his commander, and at once told him of the danger.

Captain Phipps called those about him whom he knew to be loyal. The cannons were loaded, and pointed towards the stores. The bridge connected with the shore was drawn up. As soon as the mutineers collected with a view to seize the stores, the captain hailed them and threatened to fire on them if they approached. They at once drew back, seeing that they were at a disadvantage. The stores were then brought on board under cover of the guns.

The mutineers, fearful of being left upon the barren island, threw down their arms and begged to be allowed to return to their duty. The request was granted, but Phipps took careful precautions against future mischief. He also took the first opportunity of landing the mutinous part of the crew. But in a short time he found it would be requisite to go to England to have his ship repaired. By this time, however, he had gained more precise information as to the spot where the Spanish treasure-ship had sunk. Though he was for the time baffled, he had more confidence than ever in the eventual success of his enterprise.

When he reached London he reported the result of his voyage to the officials of the Admiralty. They heard his report with apparent pleasure, but refused to intrust him with another of His Majesty's ships. England was now at war, and every ship was needed to help. So poor Phipps and his golden dreams of untold treasure were listened to with a deaf ear.

So certain was he of being able to secure the gold and silver that he appealed to the public in his effort to get sufficient means to re-embark for his El-Dorado in the west. He appealed to the public in vain at first. They laughed him to scorn. His untiring efforts at length began to tell, and after four years' perpetual talking his importunities prevailed. All those four years he had been living in the most abject poverty. Sometimes he was on the verge of starvation. But he at last succeeded. A company was formed, with the Duke of Albermarle at its head, who provided most of the funds for the outfit.

The ship arrived safely at Port de la Plata, and at once proceeded to the reef of rocks where the wreck was supposed to have occurred. The first thing was to build a very stout boat, carrying ten oars. In doing this Phipps used the adze himself. The next thing was to make a diving bell, which is said to be the first instance in which this wonderful invention was used. Phipps is credited with the invention of it; with how much truth we are not able to say. He next engaged some Indian divers, whose feats in diving were very remarkable.

The large boat was taken to the reef, the Indian divers were set to work, and the diving bell was used in exploring the bottom of the sea. Many weeks were uselessly employed in this way. Phipps' heart began to fail him as month followed month with no result. He, however, held on valiantly. In no way did his efforts ever abate. His men never saw any indication of wavering. But nerves of iron cannot stand such a strain much longer. Neither sleep nor rest could he get. His whole thoughts were converged in the one object of his life. If that hidden treasure is not found his life will be a failure, and the sea shall cover the useless body of the unsuccessful adventurer. His thoughts turned on suicide while the dark period of non-success was passing.

One day a sailor looking over the boat's side, saw a curious object that he took to be a sea-plant growing in the crevice of a rock. He told one of the Indian divers to go down and fetch it for him. On returning with the peculiar plant the red man reported that he had seen some ship's guns lying in the sand at the bottom. This startling intelligence was considered too good to be true, but further investigation proved it to be a fact.

The diving bell was now brought, and a thorough search by the whole party was made. In a short time a thrill of excitement ran through the entire company at sight of an Indian diver coolly handing up a solid bar of silver that he had found buried with the guns.

" Thanks be to God," exclaimed Phipps, "we are all made men !" The turning point in the history of the house of Mulgrave was reached. The future governors, lords-lieutenant, baronets, peers, and cabinet ministers that emanated from the Normanby family were secured.

Every effort was now made by all to bring up the discovered wealth. Diving bell and divers, sailors and officers, all went to work with a will. In a few days silver and gold to the value of three hundred thousand pounds were brought up, and Phipps set sail for England.

He and his crew arrived in London with colours flying, and hearts beating fast with joy. But their pleasure was short-lived. The king and his court needed money for wars and debauchery, and a plan was concocted among the *habitués* of the palace to urge on the king to seize all the money that Phipps had brought. It was plausibly contended that as Phipps had not accurately defined the spot where the buried wealth lay, he had wronged the king by misrepresentation. Further excuse was invented by showing that the amount of the find was enormously greater than he had ever expected it to be. Lawyers were ready to urge the illegality of a private person applying to his own fortune the flotsam and jetsam of the world's wrecks.

Better counsels, however, were brought to bear on the king, and he eventually decided to let Captain Phipps and his friends divide the whole of the find among themselves. Phipps' share was twenty thousand pounds. This was an enormous fortune for those days. It was soon decided to reward Phipps for his enterprise and honesty, and he received the honour of knighthood. A short time after the erewhile ship's carpenter was made High Sheriff of New England, and right nobly did he conduct his office. His next appointment of honour was to the Governorship of Massachusetts, where he did valiant service for his king and country, by expeditions against the French at Quebec and Port Royal.

This is the way the foundation was laid on which the opulent house of the peers of Normanby was erected. The heirs of Sir William Phipps were true chips from the old block. They increased the fortune he left them, by judicious investments. They made prudent alliances and secured lucrative positions, and in this way they are now privileged legislators for one of the greatest nations of the earth.

SIR RICHARD ARKWRIGHT.

From a wretched little underground cellar in Preston, to a lordly castle in Derbyshire. These were the two extremes in the life of Arkwright. How he effected so great a change is what we intend to tell in this sketch.

About a century ago, anyone passing along one of the narrow streets of Preston would have noticed, projecting from a cellar, a blue-and-white pole, with a tin hanging on the end of it. The notice written thereon was to the effect that Dick Arkwright would give a clean shave. But the people of that town failed to respond to the invitation of the tonsorial artist. As he stood despondingly counting his few coppers from the till one evening, a bright suggestion crossed his mind. Next morning, his competitors were startled to hear that he had boldly swung the following sign to the breeze:—

Come to the
Subterraneous Barber.
He Shaves for a Penny!!

Of course everyone knows that hitherto the regular charge had been twopence. The novelty of the sign, and the reduction in the price, soon attracted a host of customers. Before long the little shop was too small to hold all the "clients" of the enterprising barber. He thought his fortune was made, and began to put on airs accordingly. A new shop would soon be necessary, and a few assistants would be a *sine quâ non*. But, alas! for the vanity of human hopes. The ambitions of the barber's mind were quickly dispelled by a very simple process. Every barber in town displayed a notice to the effect that they also would shave for a penny.

This was really a god-send to our hero. Had his success as a cheap barber continued he might have remained a mere dexterous scraper of men's chins, and the world have suffered in consequence.

When his competitors reduced the price he followed suit—one halfpenny was now the price of a clean shave. This soon starved the poor fellow out into a more lucrative business.

When about thirty years of age he tired of starvation wages and shaving impecunious customers. So he forthwith resolved to begin business as a dealer in hair. For this purpose he travelled about to the various hiring fairs in Lancashire to buy the hair from the heads of the domestic servants. He dressed this hair himself and then disposed of it to the wig makers. As he was very quick in discovering many new methods of dressing the hair, he soon acquired the reputation among the wig makers of supplying a better article than his rivals. Among other discoveries he found out a secret for dyeing the hair in a most effective way, by which he not only made much bigger profits, but extended his trade. In a short while he was able to lay by a little money and to marry.

But his restive spirit soon saw that to make any great strides towards a fortune he must do something more than tramp around buying up tresses from servant girls.

His first efforts to improve his fortune were in a very impractical direction. As the Americans would say, he got "fooling around" the perpetual motion difficulty. This attempt to solve the insoluble not merely wasted his time, but dissipated his money. However, it was the means of ultimately leading him onwards towards the stepping stone to his millions.

He soon saw the hopelessness of the efforts. Although he left the question unsolved, the turn given to his thoughts was most valuable.

Living in a manufacturing district, where the talk of the whole population was on spinning, he soon learned the difficulty of getting sufficient weft to keep the looms employed. Up to this time all calico was woven with a cotton warp and linen weft, no method of spinning cotton with sufficient fineness and tension to form a weft having been discovered. The trade of the nation was languishing for want of weft. Customers for all the English calico that could be woven were waiting to buy it.

The idea of making a spinning machine had occurred to more than one speculator. One man near Nottingham had actually invented a machine that worked well. He perfected it, exhibited it to some friends, and then destroyed it. He thought it would take the bread out of poor people's mouths. That man, by his conscientious scruples, lost the fortune that Arkwright secured. The general opinion was that untold wealth awaited the originator of a successful spinning machine.

Arkwright soon became so engrossed in his new task of inventing this want, and so confident of ultimate success, that he neglected his regular business. He spent all his savings in purchasing materials, and getting them put together, and fell into debt and distress. His wife could see nothing in the models and machines that so occupied his time. She tried to prevent him continuing his researches. The poor woman naturally thought that her wants were more important than any discoveries. One day, while he was absent, she smashed all his models and machines, thinking she had thus rid the family of the cause of their distress. The labour of years, and the fruits of an inventive intellect, were destroyed in a moment. This outrage was more than poor Arkwright could stand. He sought and obtained a deed of separation from such a reckless helpmeet.

A visit to some rolling mills, where he saw hot bars of iron lengthened out between rollers, was the initial point of his invention. He saw that all the spinning " jennies," up to that date, only spun one thickness of thread, and that was very uneven, and had little tenacity. The thought occurred to him that if the cotton thread passed between two or three sets of rollers, each set revolving faster than the previous one, it must necessarily lengthen out the thread and twist the fibre closer.

The smashing of his models proved a good thing for him. As he had to begin anew, he left out all parts that were likely to prove unworkable, and started afresh. When he had completed the model of a machine for spinning cotton thread, he went to Preston with a man named Kay, a clockmaker from Warrington. The two were partners in the invention. Arkwright did all the headwork, and Kay put the different parts together. At this time he had not a penny to bless himself with, and was all in rags and tatters.

He was so wretchedly poor that soon after he got to Preston, when an election was taking place, the party with whom he voted had to give him a suit of clothes in which to appear at the polling-booth.

Permission to put his model into the room adjoining the Grammar School was granted. But the exhibition of his machine in a town where so many workpeople lived by the exercise of manual labour, proved a dangerous experiment. Ominous growlings were heard outside the schoolroom from time to time, and Arkwright, remembering the fate of Kay, who was mobbed and compelled to fly from Lancashire because of his invention of the fly-shuttle, wisely determined on packing up his model. He remembered poor Hargreaves, whose spinning-frame had been pulled to pieces only a short time before by a Blackburn mob, and he made up his mind to remove to a less dangerous locality.

He went accordingly to Nottingham. Poor and friendless, it may be easily supposed that Arkwright found it a hard matter to get anyone to back him in a speculation which people then looked upon as illusory. He secured a few pounds from one of the bankers in the town. That was soon spent, and further advances were refused. If that banker had possessed sufficient insight to see the merits of the poor inventor's machine, his sons to-day might have been among the richest men in England. But, nothing daunted by the refusal, Arkwright tried elsewhere for help. There was a firm of stocking weavers in the town called Need & Strutt, the latter of whom was the ingenious inventor of the stocking-frame. Mr. Strutt at once appreciated the merits of the invention. A partnership was entered into with Arkwright, whose road to fortune was now clear. The patent was secured in the name of "Richard Arkwright, of Nottingham, clockmaker." A cotton mill was built at Nottingham driven by horses. Shortly after another was erected on a larger scale, at Cromford, in Derbyshire. This was turned by a water-wheel, from which circumstance the spinning machine came to be called the water-frame.

In a year or two the success of Arkwright's inventions was fairly established. He had, however, still to perfect all the minor details. It was the subject of constant improvement, until it was eventually made practicable and profitable in an eminent degree. Success was only secured by a great deal of patience. The speculation for some years swallowed up lots of capital without much result.

When the grand results of the new method of spinning began to appear more certain, the Lancashire manufacturers fell upon Arkwright's patent to pull it to pieces, and try to rob him of the fruits of his invention. He was denounced as the enemy of the working people. A mill that he built near Chorley was destroyed by a mob while the military looked on impassively. The manufacturers in Lancashire refused to buy his materials, though they acknowledged they were the best in the market. Then they refused to pay patent right for the use of his machines, and finally combined to try and crush him in a court of law. To the eternal disgrace of our courts of justice, his patent was upset.

After the trial, when passing the hotel at which his opponents were staying, one of them said, loud enough to be heard by him : "Well, we've done the old barber at last."

He coolly replied, "Never mind, I've a razor that will shave you all." And he had.

Of course, if the large manufacturers that wove calico would not buy his thread, he must either close his factory or he must use it himself in weaving and knitting stockings. Although he had been robbed of his just rights in the patent, yet his wonderful perseverance and the undoubted value of his machine gave him such a position with the capitalists who knew him, that he soon had money enough offered on loan to start new mills for weaving and knitting. He established them in Lancashire, Derbyshire, and Scotland. He cut the ground from under the men who opposed him. He carried the war right into their own country. If they would not buy his goods he would make them up himself and sell to their customers. This very soon put a new phase on things.

The very men who had chuckled over his discomfiture were soon asking to buy his yarns. But by this time he had so distanced all his rivals that he virtually controlled the market. The man who was sneered at in the court of justice as a "mere barber adventurer," and who was to be trodden under foot by the cotton lords of Lancashire, was now the autocrat of the market. Prices were fixed by him, and he governed the main operations of the other cotton spinners. He secured two or three profits in his business, for he bought the raw material in New Orleans, spun it at Cromford in Derbyshire, wove it in Lanark, and sold it in Manchester to the large warehousemen.

At one time Arkwright was so engrossed by the labour incidental to carrying on his five works that he often had to work from four in the morning till nine at night. At fifty years of age he set to work to learn the English grammar. He was fast becoming a millionaire, yet he could barely read and write. He soon remedied this—for four years he studied hard, and practised writing when his hair was grey.

Eighteen years after constructing his first machine he began to rise into notice as a man of sterling worth. He was appointed High Sheriff of Derbyshire and soon afterwards knighted as, in his capacity of High Sheriff, he read some address to the king.

JOHN HEATHCOAT,

OF TIVERTON.

JUST a century ago, on a Derbyshire farm, near Duffield, a small boy used to tease his overworked mother by unravelling the worsted from his stockings and experimenting with self-made knitting machines. While his elder brothers were busy in robbing some neighbour's orchard, or stealing rides on their father's horses in the pasture, he was studiously manipulating wooden wheels and improvised knitting needles. The only material he could get was the worsted from his home-made socks. The poor mother was driven distracted by attempts to keep the lad's feet clad in decent socks. As a last resource, he was condemned to go barefooted.

This for a time stopped his experiments, but soon he bribed one of his brothers, by an apple, to let him unravel his stockings to obtain the coveted worsted. This was the last straw that broke the camel's back. He was packed off to school, where his vagaries were crushed out by an iron hand for a time.

It was only for a time, however. The childish love of invention, though quieted, eventually developed into one of the most useful and important of British industries. If that farmer's wife had succeeded in smothering her boy's inventive faculty, the town of Tiverton would not have become what it is to-day, and the industry of lace-making, that finds employment for some twenty thousand people, might still have remained in the hands of foreigners.

He was early removed from school and apprenticed to a frame-smith near Loughborough. The boy soon learned to handle tools with dexterity. He quickly acquired a knowledge of all the parts of which the stocking-frame is composed, as well as of the more intricate warp-machine. When he had any leisure he studied how to introduce improvements in them. When only sixteen he conceived the idea of inventing a machine by which lace might be made similar to Buckingham or French lace, then all made by hand.

The first practical improvement he succeeded in introducing was in the warp-frame. By means of an ingenious apparatus he produced "mitts" of a lacy appearance, and it was this success which decided him in pursuing the study of mechanical lace-making. The stocking-frame had already, in a modified form, been applied to the manufacture of point-net lace, but the work was unsatisfactory.

Many ingenious mechanics in Nottingham had, during a long succession of years, tried to invent a machine by which the mesh of threads should be twisted round each other. Some of these men died in abject poverty, many were driven insane and ended their gloomy days in a madhouse, jabbering of "frames" and "loops." All alike failed in the object of their search.

When Heathcoat was of age he went to Nottingham, where he soon got work at highest wages. He began as setter-up of hosiery and warp frames, and was respected for his intelligence, inventive genius, and sober conduct. Although he soon got all the work he could do, he still kept his mind on the invention that was to be the life-effort of his existence. He determined to compass the contrivance of a twist traverse-net machine.

He first of all learnt how to make Buckingham or pillow-lace by hand. While learning this art he still had to earn his living. It was a long task, needing the exercise of great perseverance and ingenuity. He wanted to contrive a machine that would make the same motions as were made by hand. His employer, Mr.

Elliott, described him at that time as inventive, patient, self-denying, and taciturn, undaunted by failures and mistakes, full of resources, and entertaining the most perfect confidence in his ultimate success. The task that had ruined scores of men and driven lots of men crazy was the problem that Heathcoat loved to solve. There was not merely the honour of the thing, there was the golden fruit of a fortune as a result.

It is almost impossible to describe an invention so complicated as the bobbin-net machine. It was a mechanical pillow for making lace, imitating in an ingenious manner the motion of the lace-maker's fingers in intersecting and tying the meshes of the lace upon her pillow.

He began his experiments by fixing common threads length-wise on a frame for the warp, then passed the weft threads between them by common pliers, and delivered them to other pliers on the opposite side; then after giving them a sideway motion and twist the threads were repassed back between the adjoining cords, the meshes being thus tied in the same way as upon pillows by hand.

He had to contrive a mechanism that should accomplish all these delicate movements. To do this cost him no small amount of mental labour. Years afterwards, in speaking of this work, he said : " The single difficulty of getting the diagonal threads to twist in the allotted space was so great that if it had to be done now I'm afraid I should not attempt it."

His next step was to provide thin metallic discs, to be used as bobbins for conducting the thread backward and forward through the warp. These discs were arranged in carrier-frames on each side of the warp.

All this time, while Heathcoat was experimenting, his wife was kept in as great anxiety as himself. Their table was spread most frugally. No time was devoted to pleasure of any kind. The entire future of the two young people was dependent on the outcome of this experimenting. Doleful examples of failure were recited to the anxious wife, and disheartening reminiscences of wrecked lives were told to the puzzled husband. His pursuit was regarded as the chimera of a disordered brain. Not a word of comfort or cheer was spoken to the indefatigable inventor.

One day, after many months of constant study, the poor wife looked at her pale-cheeked husband, and asked, " Well, will it work ?"

" No, I have had to take it all to pieces again," was the sad answer.

The poor woman could restrain her feelings no longer. She sat down and cried bitterly. She had, however, only a few more weeks to wait; for success, long worked for and well deserved, came at last. John Heathcoat was a proud and happy man when he brought home the first narrow strip of bobbin-net made by his machine, and placed it triumphantly in the hands of his wife. He knew his fortune was made, and his name would go down to posterity as a benefactor of his species.

After gaining this important success, troubles of another kind now began. As soon as the patent was proved to be most valuable, his rights as a patentee were disputed, and his claims as an inventor called in question. On the supposed invalidity of the patent, the lacemakers boldly adopted the bobbin-net machine, and set the inventor at defiance. Other patents were actually taken out for alleged improvements and adaptations. In a short while these new patentees fell out and went to law with each other, and now was the opportunity that Heathcoat seized to prove the illegality of both new patents.

The litigants were named Boville and Moore. The court was one of the high tribunals, from which there was little chance of appeal. Mr. Heathcoat secured the services of Sir John Copley (afterwards Lord Lyndhurst), and retained him for the defence in the interest of himself. " When thieves fall out honest men get their own." This was what Heathcoat wanted to bring about.

On reading over his brief Sir John confessed that he did not fully understand the merits of the case. He saw that it was of the greatest importance to his client. The labour of years and the wages to come from a life of study might be thrown away in a law court. He offered to go down into the country immediately and study the machine thoroughly until he understood it. "Then," said he, " I will defend you to the best of my ability."

That night the great lawyer took the mail for Nottingham to get up his case as counsel never got it up before. Next morning, the learned serjeant placed himself in a lace-room, and did not leave it until he could make a piece of bobbin-net lace with his own hands, and thoroughly understood the principle, as well as the details of the machine.

When the great case came on for trial, the room was crowded with interested listeners. Not merely were the lace manufacturers represented by eager hundreds, but the legal fraternity crowded in to hear and see the great legal luminary manipulate the machine which only girls are supposed to work. When the case " Boville v. Moore" was called, a model machine was lifted on to the counsel's table, and Sir John placed himself before it to explain all its principles to the Court. The fortunes of many houses depended on this speech. The welfare of several towns was involved in this supreme effort. Serjeant Copley knew this, and his efforts were correspondingly great. He worked the machine with such ease and skill, and explained the precise nature of the invention with such happy clearness, as to astonish alike judge, jury, and spectators. The thorough conscientiousness and mastery with which he handled the case had no doubt its influence upon the decision of the Court. The jury brought in a verdict that *both* the machines in question were infringements of Heathcoat's patent. The verdict was received with applause by the assembled crowd.

When the trial was over, Mr. Heathcoat knew that his fortune was made beyond a doubt. He at once began to make inquiries, and found about six hundred machines at work, all based on his patent. Of course, he proceeded to levy royalty upon the owners of them, which amounted to a large sum. The profits realised by the manufacturers were enormous. The use of the machines rapidly extended, and he received a royalty from each one.

In 1809 he established himself as a lace manufacturer at Loughborough, in Leicestershire. He carried on a good business for several years, and gave employment to a large number of workpeople, at wages varying from £5 to £10 a-week. These were glorious times for the operatives. But they soon began to lose their heads over such prosperous times. Much money made them mad. Although more hands were employed than had ever been the case before, yet it soon began to be whispered around that the machines were superseding labour. It was thought that even bigger wages might be obtained by destroying the machines, and reverting to the old system of hand-work. An extensive conspiracy was formed for the purpose of destroying them wherever found.

In 1811, disputes arose between employers and employés in the lace trade. At Sutton-in-Ashfield, a mob proceeded, at day-time, to break the frames of the manufacturers. Some of the ringleaders were punished, and for a time the open-handed destruction ceased ; but at night-time, in lonely places, many machines were wrecked by the blind folly of the workpeople. The machines were of so delicate a nature, that one blow from a hammer would destroy one, and, as the manufacture was carried on for the most part in detached buildings, remote from town, the opportunities of destroying them were very easy.

In Nottingham the Luddites were organised for the entire destruction of every machine in the kingdom. Large bodies of armed and trained men were dispatched on secret expeditions in the dead of night to go to great distances and wreck certain works. These men were under binding oaths to do the bidding of a certain ruffian, called Captain Ludd. To betray the oath or the orders of the leader was certain death. A long reign of terror was inaugurated that lasted for years, in which millions of pounds worth of property was destroyed, and thousands of innocent lives were sacrificed. Many of the mills were guarded by soldiers. All the employers were threatened. Mr. Heathcoat was doomed to death by the Luddites as being the most important manufacturer in the district. One bright sunny day in the summer of 1816, a body of rioters broke into the factory, and set fire to it with torches. They destroyed thirty-seven lace machines and £10,000 worth of property. Ten of the ringleaders were arrested, tried, condemned, and executed.

But the execution of the poor misguided wretches did not bring back the wealth that had gone up in smoke. Mr. Heathcoat made a claim upon the county for his losses. This was resisted, but the Court of Queen's Bench decided in his favour, and decreed that the county must make good his loss of £10,000. When this was paid he determined to leave such a district, where neither life nor property was safe.

At Tiverton, in Devonshire, he found a large building which had been formerly used as a woollen mill. The Tiverton cloth trade had fallen into decay, the building itself had long remained unoccupied, and the town was generally in a very poverty-stricken condition. Mr. Heathcoat bought the old mill, enlarged it, and there began the manufacture not only of lace, but the various branches connected with it—silk-spinning, yarn-doubling, net-making, and finishing. The half-decayed town began to brighten up, property soon rose in value, rents advanced, incomes of all kinds began to increase, and buildings began to loom up in the outskirts of the sleepy little place. Mr. Heathcoat wisely secured a lot of property before starting his works. He bought it at a mere song when it was difficult to find a purchaser. As soon as the various factories were in running order he had big offers for some of his recent purchases, but he held on. The next step was to start a large iron foundry, and then he began a manufactory for agricultural implements. More workpeople came flocking in to the little town. Houses were in great demand at good rents. Shops were started and building sites advanced in value.

It was a favourite idea of his that steam-power should be applied to ploughing. In 1832 he invented and patented a steam plough that was a good success. His works were soon giving employment to over 2,000 people, all of whom regarded Mr. Heathcoat more as a father than a master. He built schools at a cost of £6,000 and endowed them. For thirty years he represented Tiverton in Parliament. At the age of seventy-seven he went down to his rest, leaving behind him a character for probity, manliness, and mechanical genius, of which his descendants may well be proud.

———

THOMAS GUY,

The Founder of a Hospital.

LONDON is indebted to stock gambling for one of its finest charities. The little bookseller, who filched a third of a million from the pockets of the dupes, soothed his conscience by devoting it to charity.

Thomas Guy was born in Tooley-street when horses and cattle grazed on one side of it, when men were hung for burning coal instead of wood, and when all the houses of London were, built of wood. His father died when Thomas was eight years old, and his widowed mother had hard work to provide an education for her boy. But the lad, as soon as he was able to read, devoured every book that came within his reach. Instead of helping to find food for himself and mother, he spent all his time in reading. The knowledge thus acquired came in useful in after-life. It was seemingly a poor investment at the time, but it paid well in the end. The poor woman, who fretted to see her boy spending day after day and month after month poring over books, while she was wearing out her health to get a living, was well rewarded by the enormous wealth that he afterwards accumulated.

He was apprenticed when sixteen years old to a bookseller in Cheapside. After serving his time, he was elected a member of the Stationers' Company. But before his time was up a circumstance happened that helped him wonderfully in his upward career. One fine morning in September, 1666, as he stood in the shopdoor, he saw the smoke of a great fire come sweeping over the street, and as it was fanned by a strong wind the wooden structures consumed like so much tinder. For four days it raged; the sky was like the top of a burning furnace, visible for forty miles around. The crackling of the flames, the shrieking of women, the fall of towers, houses, and churches, was like a terrible tornado. The houses in four hundred streets were burnt to the ground, nearly one hundred churches were destroyed, and property to the value of £10,000,000 was wasted. The Great Plague, however, which was raging at the time, and which had killed seventy thousand people in London, was burnt out by the Great Fire. The narrow streets and clumsy houses of old London were replaced by broader thoroughfares and stone buildings.

Guy's master was ruined by the loss of his shop and books. But Guy, being only a shopman, suffered no serious injury. As soon as the streets were rebuilt, he rented a small shop, and with his small savings started as bookseller. He did well from the very first. The position of his shop almost guaranteed success. It was situated at the sharp corner formed by Cornhill and Lombard-street, looking out on Poultry and Cheapside, and near the Royal Exchange.

Charles Knight says of him: "Placed thus, in the very heart of the great commercial operations of London, I can see the shadow of the young bookseller as he sits in his shop amidst his small stock, restless at the want of occupation, and envying the great merchant adventurers congregating in the Exchange. He spreads his new books and his old upon a board in front of his window, now and then soliciting the busy trader who glances at them to buy Mr. Wingate's 'Arithmetic Made Easy,' or Mr. Record's 'Grounds of Art,' or 'The Old and Tedious Way of Numbering Reduced to a New and Brief Method.' He had divinity books, too ; theology was by far the most exciting topic of those days. He meditated frequently upon the large trade that he could command if it were in his power to offer godly people bibles well printed and cheap."

There was no such commodity to be had in England. All the arts associated with the production of books were hampered with privileges and restrictions, and were very inferior to those practised abroad under conditions of freedom. The privilege of printing bibles was a monopoly only enjoyed by the king's printer and Oxford University. The printing had come to be so bad that the letters were hardly legible, and the bibles were full of gross blunders. One text was printed: "Know ye not that the *un*righteous shall inherit the kingdom of God."

Guy made up his mind that to supply better bibles would be the sure way to make a fortune. He sent an agent to Holland, who bought for him good paper and fine types, and intrusted them to competent Dutch printers. In this way good bibles were produced, and sent over to the shop in Cornhill. They were sold in great numbers, and at a big profit. He had to smuggle them into England under all kinds of disguises. The favourite plan was to pack them up in cases and label them "gin." He was vigorously fined for selling them, but he could afford to pay his fines and still make a large profit.

Other booksellers followed his device, and soon the trade became so notorious that the Government interfered and seized on all the foreign bibles that they could find. The dealers were harassed and punished until the trade was entirely stopped. But Guy had had the cream off the business, and saved money while it lasted. All his competitors quitted the pursuit, as they thought it too risky. By this time Guy was a man of some position in the business world of London. He was able to make a proposition to the University of Oxford to buy out their monopoly. The offer was accepted, and he now was able to do a much larger trade and at much greater profits. He bought his type in Holland and his paper in England, and proceeded to print his own bibles on a larger scale than had ever been attempted before. He began to make his fortune now in good earnest, and to aid the literature of the times by issuing well-printed bibles at a lower price.

E

He was a miserly man.   While most fortune-hunters look upon marriage as a means to help them, he seemed to think his surest way to accumulate a fortune was to keep single.   All the household work of his little establishment he did himself.   His rank penuriousness soon obtained for him the name of " miser."

Such profits as he got, and such a trade as he did, with such small expenses, were bound to enrich him.   In a few years he ventured on the luxury of a female servant, and now came the only romance of his life.   Charles Knight says of him : " He is lonely.   He has indulged himself with the cost of a female servant, who cooks his frugal meals and keeps his holland shirt tidy.   But he wants the solace of a household friend.   He has once or twice conversed, during the banquet at Guildhall, with the daughter of a rich stationer, and has found her deplorably ignorant of the commodities in which her father deals.   Gradually he begins to think that his own maidservant is quite as attractive as a citizen's daughter.   What if this neat-handed Phyllis should become his wife !   He is sure that he can compel her to regulate his affairs with due economy.   She has professed that implicit obedience to his will that he requires.   He at last makes his proposal, and is accepted.   But there is one danger that the hand-maiden has not seen.   She has not thought of the dire offence of having an opinion of her own in opposition to his.   The workman engaged in repairing the pavement near the door, in Guy's absence, is told by her to do some extra work which Guy had not ordered.   The workman hesitates.   She little knows what she is doing when she says, ' Do as I wish.   Tell him I bade you, and I am sure he will not be angry.'   The poor girl must accept her destiny, to remain unmarried to the thriving bookseller.   The romance of Thomas Guy's life is over."   He refuses to wed the girl who would be guilty of such extravagance.

The great effort of his life was yet to be made.   The million was still to be reached.   In 1711 the Lord Treasurer, finding the State burdened with a debt of £10,000,000, hit upon the audacious expedient of having a national buccaneering navy, the State creditors to be the only recipients of the boundless wealth that was to be stolen on the South Seas.   He procured an Act of Parliament appointing that, " to the intent that the trade to the South Seas be carried on for the increase of the wealth of this realm, a company should be formed with the exclusive right of trading and fighting from Tierra-del-Fuego to Brazil."   The company was to be aided by the British army in its nefarious proceedings.   Very soon its power and wealth enabled it to buy up the whole of the National Debt and issue paper money to liquidate it.   This was the beginning of the South Sea Bubble.   Stock-jobbing now commenced for the first time.   The shares in the company were offered at £100, and were quickly in demand at

£150. As soon as the public found that there was to be a profit got out of buying shares and selling them again at an advance, everyone was eager to taste of the good things offered. Men bought the shares at any price that was asked and simply held them for a few days and sold out at an advance. In a short time they were quoted at £500. Such rapid advances as these induced others to start companies. No sooner were the shares issued than there were countless applications for them. It was no matter what the purpose of the company might be, everyone was willing to buy the shares simply to gamble with them. Any impudent impostor, while the delusion was at its height, needed only to hire a room at some coffee-house for a few hours and open a subscription book for shares in something relative to some hare-brained scheme, having first advertised in the papers of the preceding day, and he might, in a few hours, find subscribers for one or two millions of imaginary stock.

At one time the South Sea £100 shares were to be sold for £1,000, and the shares of a Welsh copper company, without having a penny of real capital, originally valued at £4, could hardly be bought for £95. Some of the companies went so far as ten millions of capital, and none were less than a million. One was designed to make salt water fresh; another, to discover perpetual motion; a third, "to import jackasses from Spain, in order to propagate a larger kind of mules in England;" and a fourth, "for the invention of melting sawdust and chips, and casting them into clean deal boards, without cracks or knots."

Of course the bubble burst ere long, and great was the consternation as shares began to fall. Some of the prices tumbled from £500 in the morning to £20 in the afternoon.

As South Sea shares were first beginning to be issued, Thomas Guy bought a great number at a low figure. He held on to these as they were advancing. Offers were made to him that would have netted a handsome fortune, but he would not sell. While still a large dealer in government securities, he was not above the low calling of a "shaver" of seamen's pay tickets. The needy agents of James II., following an example of long standing, were in the habit of paying the seamen of the Royal Navy, not in cash, but in promissory notes, for which cash was to be given at a distant day. As the poor men required their money at once, it was usual for them to sell their pay tickets as soon as they were received. Guy is said to have found it a very lucrative business to buy their tickets and make a profit of about 60 to 100 per cent. per annum upon them. He would give the poor fellows two-thirds of their nominal value, holding them till they became due, and he could recover the whole amount from the Government.

In 1710, just when the South Sea Company was coming into favour, and when its £100 shares were to be bought for £120

each, he was possessed of £45,000 worth of its stock. Part of
this he sold when the shares were worth £300 apiece. The rest
he kept for a few years, and sold out when he could get £600 for
each of them. By this transaction he cleared £150,000. When
the great bubble burst he did not own a share.

Having become wealthy, he entered Parliament and sat for
about twelve years as member for Tamworth. In 1705, he built
and endowed some almshouses there. In 1707, he added three
new wards to St. Thomas's Hospital, in Southwark, and other
minor charities were done by him all through the time of his
prosperity.

But his greatest act of charity, and his boldest scheme of duping
the unwary, was reserved to the last. In 1720, when he was
seventy-six, he made a speculation in a lot of shares at a mere
nominal price. He then set to work, with others, to puff the
value up by all kinds of lying and newspaper deceit. The
dividends were paid out of principal, and prices were quoted of
fictitious sales from one member of the ring to another at
enormous advances. For a time the investors and the smaller
speculators were almost crazy to get hold of the stock. None of
it was allowed to be sold for some time to outside parties. This
made the people more anxious to buy them. At last the
suppositious value was high enough for the conspirators, and Guy
"unloaded" at a nett profit of a third of a million. This ill-
gotten gain was used to quieten his conscience and immortalise his
name by founding a hospital near to London Bridge.

C. M. PALMER, M.P.

In 1850, Jarrow-on-Tyne was a village of about eight hundred
inhabitants. To-day it is the most flourishing town in the North
of England, with forty thousand population. This enormous
growth is entirely due to one man, who started a small ship-
building yard there in 1852. About sixty hands were employed
at that time. Over six thousand now are at work in this yard.

Charles Palmer was born at South Shields in the year 1822, and
attended Dr. Bruce's school in Newcastle. The venerable schoolmaster often visits his pupil, and delights in recalling the ob-
streperous acts of his young days. The grey-headed Doctor
recounts with glee the first time he subdued his pupil's mischievous
pranks, and tells with evident joy the pride he felt at shaking
hands with his bright pupil as he left the school to make his way
in the world. "I always knew that Charles would make his
mark in the world," said Dr. Bruce. The mischievous Newcastle

schoolboy is now one of the wealthiest men in England. He has obtained his wealth by fair means, and while enriching himself has benefited his neighbours, his town, and his country.

Mr. Palmer's father was a shipowner, who gave his boy a good education, and afterwards helped him to start in business for himself. The lad seems to have been a born merchant, for his every step was a success. When only twenty-three years of age he joined Sir William Hutt, John Bowes, and Nicholas Wood in a venture of manufacturing coke. This soon branched out into a coalmining business as well. The coal was dug out of a mine that the partners bought, and burnt into coke for iron smelting. As the mine developed, more coal was brought to the surface than could be profitably coked. The partners regretted their inability to dispose of all the coal, and contemplated reducing the output. They never dreamt of being able to sell their surplus in London. The coalfields in the south held a monopoly of that trade through being so much nearer. All the coal was carried by rail to London except such small quantities as the coasting colliers carried.

The very necessities of the case developed a plan that made Palmer's millions. The carriage on a ton of coals to the metropolis was greater than the value of the coals. The railway charges were exorbitant, and the sea voyage was slow and risky. The thought occurred to Mr. Palmer that to compete successfully with the steam-power on land he must use steam-power on the sea. He commenced the business of iron shipbuilder simply with the object of carrying out this idea. An iron screw-steamer, named the *John Bowes*, was accordingly designed, built, launched, and sent forth upon her first voyage. Like every other innovator, Mr Palmer had to encounter much opposition and ridicule. Wiseacres shook their heads, and argued "that it would be impossible for steamers carrying 650 tons of coal, and costing about £10,000, to compete with vessels that consumed no fuel, and which, though carrying only half the quantity, cost little more than £1,000, or only one-tenth the amount."

But Palmer was not the man to be turned aside by short-sighted, prejudiced statements, even though uttered by influential men. He felt assured that he was on the right track in this matter. But even he little thought where the thing would land him. On her first voyage—which many, of course, prophesied would also be her last—the *John Bowes*, the first screw-collier, was laden with five hundred tons of coal in four hours. She steamed at the rate of nine miles an hour, and reached London in forty-eight hours from her departure. In thirty hours she discharged her cargo, and in forty-eight hours more she was again in the Tyne. So that in five days she performed, successfully, an amount of work that would have taken two average-sized sailing colliers more than a month to accomplish.

The jeers of the supercilious critics' were for ever silenced. The man who accomplished such a quiet revolution began to be spoken of. His fame caused orders to pour in upon him faster than he could undertake them, not only from private individuals and public companies, but from the English and foreign governments.

He was now at the head of three separate businesses, the coking, the coalmining, and iron shipbuilding. Such cheap carriage on coal soon advanced the value of all property in his neighbourhood. The coalmine was worked to its utmost capacity, night and day. Every ton could be sold at good profit. He killed three birds with one stone. He established a new and paying industry, he increased the value of his land and mines, and he made his coalmine one of the most profitable in the North of England.

The restless energy of his mind did not allow him to be contented with the grand success he had already achieved. His next step was to lease a thousand acres from Lord Normanby, and dig his own iron. For this purpose he actually constructed a port at a cost of £40,000, and named it Port Mulgrave. His next step was to buy large limestone quarries, and now he had the whole production of a steamer, from the iron ore to the iron plates.

He soon added other branches to those already established, such as blast-furnaces, forges, engine-works, and bridge-yards. When everything was complete he could turn out a fully-equipped steamer, every item of which had been produced by his own works, no one but himself having had any profit out of the construction.

The first Admiralty contract that he obtained was the *Terror*, an iron-clad of 2,000 tons. This was built in three and a-half months, and Mr. Palmer said " she would have been completed in three months had not the declaration of peace slackened the energies of the men, which up to that date had been so nobly maintained by their patriotic feeling."

Mr. Palmer disputes with Sir John Brown the position of first introducer of rolled plates on men-of-war-ships. He says : " We built a target 9 feet square. The cells were filled with compressed cotton, which we had found very effective in stopping shot. On this target was a thin teak backing, and on the teak were bolted one hammered and two rolled plates. The target was bolted on to the side of an old wooden frigate at Portsmouth. The first shot fired missed the target, went through both sides of the frigate, and to my astonishment skimmed over the surface of the water for nearly a mile. The firing showed that whilst the hammered plates split and cracked to pieces the rolled plates were not broken, only indented. The commander in charge of the experiments was so well pleased that he recommended a series of experiments to be tried. The Admiralty were willing, but required us to provide targets at our own expense. Having already spent £1,000 for the good of the country we declined the proposal. Nevertheless, we had proved to the Admiralty the important fact that rolled iron was best, and we soon profited by it."

Mr. Palmer built most of the National Line of steamers and owns a great interest in them. He built most of the Guion Line, and has a large share in them. He helped to establish the new route to India *via* Brindisi.

After his various works were established, he sold out to a limited company for two million pounds, and retains the management to this day. He employs twelve thousand men in all parts of England and Wales. He has mines in Northumberland, Durham, and Wales. The output of his collieries is two million and three-quarter tons annually.

And so the formerly almost " deserted village" rapidly assumed an importance in the commercial world. A new spirit was infused into the place by Palmer. Workmen hastened to the place in hundreds; tradesmen followed in large numbers. The sound of the forge, the whirr of machinery, the whistle of steam engines, and the ceaseless stroke of the riveters' hammers, fell like a new voice upon the ear of Tyneside, and proclaimed that one of her sons had brought her fresh glory.

SIR JOHN SINCLAIR,

THE man who made a road ten miles long in ten hours, was originally a country laird, born to a considerable estate situated near John-o'-Groat's House, almost beyond the reach of civilisation, in a wild country fronting the North Sea. His father died while he was a youth of sixteen, and the management of the family property thus early devolved upon him. When only eighteen he began a course of vigorous improvements in the county of Caithness, which eventually spread all over Scotland. The small farmers of Caithness were so poor that they could scarcely afford to keep a horse. The hard work was chiefly done, and the burdens borne, by the women. If a cottier lost a horse it was usual for him to marry, a wife being cheaper than a horse. The country was without roads or bridges. Drovers driving their cattle south had to swim the rivers along with their cattle. The main track leading into Caithness lay along a high shelf on a mountain side, the road being several hundred feet of perpendicular height above the sea, which dashed below.

Sir John, although only a lad of eighteen, determined to make a new road over the hill of Ben Cheilt. He received no assistance from the other proprietors; they regarded him and his schemes with incredulity and derision. But he knew that to get the full benefit out of his estate, there must be an improvement in the means of locomotion. He saw that every acre of his vast estate would double in value by a few improvements of a radical nature. He laid out the road himself, assembled some twelve hundred workmen early one summer morning, set them simultaneously to work, superintended their labours, stimulated them by his example, and, before night, what had been a dangerous sheep-track, ten miles in length, scarcely passable for led horses, was made a good carriage road, as if by the power of magic.

Never before had ten miles of road been made in ten hours. When the neighbouring landowners heard of it, they rode over to view what they believed to be merely some childish work of a temporary nature that the first rain would undo. But the incredulity pictured on their stolid countenances gradually evaporated as they rode over the well-built road. A mere boy had awakened them from their "sleepy hollow," and the benefits that shortly accrued from this grand example soon set others to work. More roads were made, bridges were built, corn mills were erected, and waste lands inclosed and improved.

The estate that three or four years before had barely afforded enough for the Sinclairs to live upon, was now yielding a good rental. All the money obtained from increased rents was expended in improvements. Improved methods of culture were introduced, and regular rotation of crops. Premiums to encourage better industry were awarded. Every penny that he could raise was put into improvements. The good that he was doing had its effect upon his neighbours. They soon saw the benefits that Sir John reaped, and hastened to follow his example. From being one of the most inaccessible districts of the north, Caithness became a pattern county for its roads, its agriculture, and its fisheries. In Sinclair's youth the post was carried by a runner once a-week. The young baronet then declared that he would never rest till a coach drove daily to Thurso. The people did not look forward to any such thing, and it became a proverb in the county to say, "Ou, ay, that will happen when Sir John sees the daily mail at Thurso!" But Sir John *did* see his dream realised. In a very few years the daily mail was established to Thurso.

As time rolled on his rents increased, and he became one of the richest men in his county, but he made up his mind to increase his fortune still more by improving the quality of the sheep that were raised in Caithness. For this purpose he imported 800 sheep from nearly every country in the world at an enormous expense. These he assorted, selecting those with the best qualities for the purpose of in-breeding with the native flocks. The result was the introduction into all parts of Scotland of the celebrated Cheviot breed.

Sheep farmers scouted the idea of south country flocks being able to thrive in the far north. But Sinclair persevered, and in a few years there were 300,000 Cheviots in the four northern counties. The value of grazing land was thus immensely increased. Northern estates which before were comparatively worthless rose in the market to a big figure.

He was elected to Parliament, and induced Mr. Pitt to establish the Board of Agriculture, which soon was felt throughout the kingdom by its influence in redeeming tens of thousands of acres from barrenness. He was the founder of the celebrated fisheries at Wick and Thurso. He urged on Parliament for many years, and at last succeeded in obtaining, the inclosure of a harbour for Wick, which is now probably the greatest and most prosperous fishing town in the world.

In 1793 the stagnation produced by the war led to an unusual number of bankruptcies, and many of the first houses in Manchester and Glasgow were tottering, because the usual sources of credit were closed up. Intense distress was imminent among the working classes. Sir John urged in Parliament that Exchequer notes to the amount of £5,000,000 should be issued immediately as a loan to such merchants as would give security. The suggestion was adopted. The vote was passed late at night, and early next morning Sir John, anticipating the delays of red-tapeism, went to bankers in the city and borrowed £70,000, which he dispatched the same evening to the north. Pitt met Sir John in the House and expressed his regret that the money could not be sent off for several days. "It is already gone; it left London by to-night's mail," was Sir John's triumphant reply; and in afterwards relating the anecdote he added, with a smile of pleasure, "Pitt was as much startled as if I had stabbed him."

JOSEPH COWEN,

The Radical M.P.

It will surprise most of our readers to learn that the democratic Joseph Cowen is a millionaire. It is natural to associate a slim purse with democracy. The broad-shouldered man, with short coat and wide-brimmed soft felt hat, that can be seen walking from the Strand down the right-hand side of Essex-street, to his office in the far corner, would not be taken for one of the wealthiest men in England; but he is.

When Parliament is in session, a hansom cab generally draws up at the door of the office in the corner about two o'clock in the morning. "Our London Correspondent" of the *Newcastle*

Chronicle alights, rushes upstairs, and proceeds to dictate a
London Letter to the young fellow at the end of the "special
wire." That long message will be read by forty thousand people
in a few hours, and it will help to make history. The policy of a
Cabinet may be changed by that message, as it has been in a
critical moment in our history.

Mr. Cowen is not merely a member of Parliament and newspaper proprietor—he is also a colliery owner, fire-brick manufacturer, and retort maker. He is popularly supposed by his
neighbours to be worth a clear million, and we intend to give our
readers some slight idea of how this was made.

His father, Sir Joseph Cowen, was a working blacksmith in his
young days. He used to forge links in a chain shop, at a village
called Winlaton, in Durham. When standing by his anvil,
earning his bread by the power of his muscle, his brain was active
in studying out some method of raising himself. He saw that
the mere producers of wealth never shared in its accumulation;
he was soon convinced that to be something more than a mere
machine for others to employ, he must move to a place with
greater opportunities. He went to work at the engine-shops of
Hawkes & Co., at Gateshead. As soon as he had thoroughly
learnt all that he could profitably use, he left, and joined another
man, as ambitious as himself, and began making bricks, at
Blaydon, on a small scale. He and his partner worked hard and
lived frugally for the first few years; every penny they saved was
devoted to improving their business.

At this time, Newcastle and Gateshead were extending rapidly.
As the mines were more developed, and coal became cheaper, ironworks were built, and shipping became an important industry on
the Tyne. Houses of all kinds were in demand, and builders were
glad to get Cowen's bricks, which soon became known for their
superiority. As the demand increased, the partners extended
their yards, and became known as substantial business men. At
this time, a new industry was started. Hitherto it had been
customary to smelt iron with coal or charcoal, but it was found
much better to use coke, and fire-bricks were in great demand for
building the coke ovens with. Mr. Cowen seized on the
opportunity to investigate the best method of making the bricks
needed. He found, after careful experiments, that the clay lying
below the coal strata was best for the purpose, and at once made
arrangements for going into the business on an enormous scale.
The more he made, the larger the demand got to be. He adopted
the plan of stamping all his bricks with his name and address.
Soon Cowen's bricks were the standard in the market. His next
step upward was to buy a coalmine, and dig his own coal and
clay. He now had all the profit of the business in his own firm,
and the wealth began to accumulate fast.

Mr. Cowen had now proved himself a man of successful enterprise. He saw that the future of the business was likely to be very profitable, and he disliked the idea of having a partner to share the profits. With this view he bought out his brother-in-law, and launched out in a bigger way than ever. He obtained a gold medal at the first Exhibition in 1851, which caused quite an excitement in the business. About this time he introduced his fire-clay gas retorts, which would stand a greater heat than any others made. These were bought for the gas companies that were being started in nearly every town.

The River Tyne was a wretched stream compared to what it is to-day; it was a brawling current, with rocks, shoals, and other impedimenta. The main craft using it were mere fishing boats and small colliers. Cowen saw the importance of clearing away the rocks and dredging the mud. By lowering the bed of the stream large ships and powerful steamers could come up to Newcastle and to Blaydon. The railway carriage to the seaport would be saved, and property of all kinds would advance in value. To do this Mr. Cowen joined other influential men and petitioned Parliament for a River Tyne Commission, with power to spend large sums on the improvement of the stream. The commission was appointed, and Mr. Cowen was elected chairman and made a life member.

For his praiseworthy action in this matter he received a knighthood. He was elected member of Parliament for Newcastle, and his high position enabled him to advance his business prospects in many ways. Sir Joseph Cowen, the brickmaker, received larger orders than plain Mr. Cowen. There were not many titled men in business at that time, and it was a novelty to see an invoice "Bought of Sir Joseph Cowen"—"so many thousand bricks."

He was not satisfied until the Tyne was navigable three miles above Newcastle; right to the doors of his numerous works. When he built a wharf and had steamers of his own loading from his yards, one of the ambitions of his life was accomplished.

The Cowen family never looked back after this. All the material needed in their manufactures was obtained and manipulated on their own property; it was shipped from their own wharf in their own boats, and every cent of profit was theirs.

This was the origin of the present fortune. The younger Joseph Cowen has added to it immensely. He was born in 1831, and after a good education in a local school went to Edinburgh University, when Christopher North was still lecturing. Young Cowen having no profession in view, simply sought culture here. He met Mazzini in the northern city, and established a lifelong friendship with the Italian patriot. He exposed and denounced Sir Joseph Graham both by pen and tongue for tampering with the exile's letters. The influence of the noble-hearted Mazzini induced him to become a member of the revolutionary party that had for its object the downfall of every tyrant in Europe. He acted as agent for Polish, Hungarian, Italian, and French refugees in forwarding their correspondence to their respective countries. He gave them for months at a time the hospitality of his home at Blaydon.

In 1874 Cowen was elected to Parliament. A few years after, when the proposition to add " Empress " to the grand old title of Queen was made, there was such a burst of oratory from the member for Newcastle as startled the listening House of Commons. It was no astonishment to Newcastle when he rose up in the House and electrified it with his eloquence. Newcastle had heard many a speech as brilliant and as telling as the one he there gave. This speech made his reputation. It was the talk of the clubs and the drawing-rooms. The discovery that oratory is not dying out was the theme of editorial pens, and Cowen was the hero of the hour.

In 1863, there was a weakly paper struggling for existence called the *Newcastle Daily Chronicle.* Mr. Cowen bought it from Messrs. Lambert. For a time he wrote many of the leading articles, and personally superintended the paper. In a very short time the circulation jumped up from a few thousands to 20,000 a-day. The offices were soon removed to a more extensive building, and a special wire was erected to connect the Newcastle office with a London establishment. When Mr. Cowen went to represent Newcastle in Parliament, and sent those London Letters to his paper, the circulation doubled in a short while, and to-day it has one of the largest circulations of any daily paper out of London.

Some time ago the train service from London was so arranged that the London papers could be sold in York, Middlesboro', Darlington, and Stockton at an earlier hour than the Newcastle papers. There was danger of Cowen's paper losing its circulation in those towns if something was not done. He at once arranged with the railway company for a special train at a very early hour. There is now a *Chronicle* train that runs fifty miles just to carry this one newspaper, a thing unknown in newspaper enterprise before.

Hatton, in reckoning up our hero, says he is " frank, stubborn, clear-headed, tender-hearted, slow to wrath ; but, being roused, an ugly customer."

SIR ROBERT PEEL.

THE fortune that the Peels now enjoy was started by a small farmer near Blackburn. There is a long, low building on the bleak Lancashire soil, called Hole House Farm, where a certain yeoman, named Robert Peel, used to try and make a living for himself, his wife, and his numerous sons. The barren land did not yield very well, and he was compelled to have a few looms in the house and weave calico. The very beginning of his success dates from his adopting the new invention called the carding cylinder. His trade was very small at first. He used to buy his warp and weft on credit, weave it up at home, take it to market on a donkey's back, and sell it for as much as he could get. When the newest invention of a carding cylinder came out, his neighbours were either too poor or too timorous to buy one. He got one, and began to make a little money. Pretty soon he was sufficiently forehanded to pay cash for his warp and weft, and by that means he got them cheaper. As his boys grew up he got more looms, and was eventually quite a thriving man for that date.

But he used this comparative success only as a stepping-stone to a greater effort. His attention was soon directed to calico *printing*, at that time almost an unknown art. The experiments were secretly conducted in his own house. Peel took a pewter plate, such as he used at meals, and sketched a pattern of a parsley leaf upon it by means of a sharp-pointed instrument. This figure he filled up with colour rubbed into it. In a cottage at the end of the farmhouse lived a woman who kept a calendering machine. Going into her cottage, he put the plate, with the colour rubbed into the figured part and some calico over it, through the machine, when it was found to leave a satisfactory impression. This was the origin of roller-printing on calico; and this was the starting point of the present wealthy firm of Peels.

Stimulated by such success, Robert Peel gave up farming, removed to Brookside, and devoted himself exclusively to printing calicoes. There, with the aid of his sons, who were as energetic as himself, he successfully carried on the trade for several years.

The great Sir Robert Peel left his father when only nineteen years of age, and borrowed £500 from a Mr. Yates to start business for himself. He took Yates' son in as partner. He found all the experience; his partner provided the money. An old ruined cornmill, with a few acres of ground, was purchased near Bury, and the two men built a cheap wooden shed, and started business on their own account.

The careful manner in which the partners lived may be inferred from the following incident in their early career: Peel lodged with Yates, and paid him eight shillings a-week; but Yates, thinking this too little, asked for an increase of a shilling a-week, to which Peel demurred, and a quarrel between the partners took place, which was compromised by Peel paying an advance of sixpence a-week.

Yates' eldest child was a girl called Ellen. She soon became an especial favourite with the young lodger. On returning from his day's work, he would take the girl upon his knee, and say to her, "Nellie, thou bonny little lass, wilt be my wife?" The child of course would answer "Yes." "Then I'll wait for thee, Nellie; I'll wed thee and none else." And Robert Peel did wait. As the girl grew in beauty towards womanhood, his love for her strengthened. At the end of ten years they were married, Mrs. Peel being only seventeen years of age. The pretty child whom her mother's lodger had nursed upon his knee became eventually Lady Peel, the mother of the future Prime Minister of England. London fashionable life proved injurious to her health. She only lived three years after the title had been conferred upon her husband. Old Mr. Yates used afterwards to say, "If Robert hadn't made our Nellie a lady, she might ha' been living yet."

One of the secrets of Peel's grand success was bought by him from a commercial traveller for a mere song. This is a process called *resist work* in calico printing. It is accomplished by the use of paste on such parts of the cloth as are intended to remain white. The beauty of its effect, and the extreme precision of the outline in the pattern produced, at once placed the Bury establishment at the head of all the factories for printing in the country. Soon the Peels started other places for working this process at several different towns in the north of England, and to-day they stand pre-eminent in their line of business.

JOHN RYLANDS,
OF MANCHESTER.

THE father of the Manchester millionaire was originally a hand-loom weaver at Parr, near St. Helens. He rose to be manager and partner of a small factory, and eventually opened a draper's shop in St. Helen's, where the bulk of the goods produced at the little factory was sold. The plan of being both manufacturer and retailer soon told its tale in his banking account. He gradually rose to be known as a substantial business man.

His three sons were taught to fight their own way in the world and expect no help from their father. John was the youngest and the best scholar of the three. He seems to have been a money-maker even when a boy. When about fourteen, he spent his pocket-money in buying a lot of trinkets put up at an auction sale. Having sold these at a good profit he found himself with an unusually large sum of money in his pocket. He told his good luck to an old woman who had nursed him in infancy. She and her husband had been hand-loom weavers.

"Why don't you buy a little warp and weft with the money you've got, and let us weave them?" she said.

John took quite a fancy to the suggestion, bought some material for the old dame to work up, and the investment proving profitable continued to employ her. He thus became both a manufacturer and merchant in a small way, though still a schoolboy.

After school hours he acted as assistant in his father's shop, and earned quite a good wage for a boy. By the time his schooling was over, he was promoted to be regular assistant at a large salary for those times. His earnings and his holidays he spent in weaving. All his savings were put into warp and weft, and before he was seventeen he had several families employed working up his material.

There was no romance in such a beginning as this, but there was promise of a great success so far as accumulation of wealth goes. His eldest brother, Joseph, started a mill in Wigan, and did wonderfully well. In 1821 he had succeeded so far as to ask John, then only eighteen, to join him as partner and act as commercial traveller for the firm. He entered into the arrangement, and started out on horseback with his samples fastened on to the saddle. His journeys were mostly to the towns in Lancashire, Yorkshire, Cheshire, and North Wales. His patterns were principally ginghams, calicoes, and other cotton goods. He proved himself a successful traveller, and used to make it his boast that he never tried to sell to a man without succeeding sooner or later.

The two brothers soon built up a larger trade than they had capital for, and their father offered to become a third partner, and find more capital. The result was the establishment of the now famous firm of Rylands & Sons. At this time they had weaving mills at Wigan and St. Helens, and a large draper's shop in St. Helens.

Chester was then a larger place than Manchester, so far as trading went. The Rylands used to send all their goods by carts to Chester.

In 1822 John said to his brother, "Instead of sending goods to Chester fair, let us send them to Manchester fair, and open a warehouse in that town."

The suggestion was a good one, and soon carried out. In a few weeks a house in High-street was rented and filled with cotton goods. John removed there and lived on the premises, and made this the centre of his business operations. His first house in the metropolis of Cottondom was not so grand as his present one.

At this date all calicoes were woven with a linen warp. The Rylands soon began to buy their linen direct from the flax-growers and spinners in the North of Ireland, thus saving any intermediary profits. As their capital increased they added other branches to their business, such as dyeing and printing.

In 1824 they found it would be necessary to enlarge their works. With this view they bought two large estates near Wigan—one containing dyeing and bleaching works; on the other they built a spinning mill for producing both cotton and linen yarn. This was, reckoned a tremendous establishment when it was opened, but in comparison with their present factories is small.

The purchase of these estates was the gigantic stride that landed John Rylands among the millionaires of the world. As it happened, there was a rich vein of coal underlying part of the land, that was useful for both domestic and manufacturing purposes. A colliery was soon sunk, and the house coal was sold, while the coarser kinds they consumed in their works. In this way all the coal dealers' and colliery proprietors' profits were saved, and the firm was able to devote more capital to their already enormous trade.

Joseph Rylands retired from the firm in 1840, and went into business in Hull. Soon after John and his father bought a large cotton mill at Ainsworth, where they now spin about twenty tons of cotton a-week, and weave 30,000 lbs of calico. Nearly 1,000 operatives are employed in this one mill alone.

In 1847, the old man died, leaving John as the sole representative of Rylands & Sons. Unhampered now by any partners, and having plenty of capital and almost unlimited credit, he launched out larger than ever. The warehouse in High-street was enlarged, and other branches of mercantile business were added, until a draper could furnish himself completely out of Rylands' stock. He was thus the producer of nearly all that he sold, right from the coal mine, the flax field, the spinning mill, the weaving shed, the bleach works, the dye works, the printing works, up to the dealer's warehouse. He saved eight or nine profits, and paid out nothing for distributing his goods.

By 1864, his profits had so increased in his hands that he was able to buy some large cotton mills at Gorton, which he enlarged and made into one of the largest factories in England. They cover 16,000 square yards, and employ 1,600 hands. In 1865, he built a larger factory near Wigan, known as the Gidlow Works. This magnificent mill is fireproof. The top room is for receiving cotton, brought from the railway over a viaduct 300 feet long. The second floor contains the machinery for cleaning, opening, and making-ready for the cardroom. The bottom floor is for boilers and engines. It contains 60,000 spindles, and produces 75,000 lbs. of yarn weekly. Rylands' three mills at Gidlow, Gorton, and Ainsworth give employment to 5,000 people.

SIR JOSIAH MASON,
THE PENMAKER.

THREE hundred and fifty thousand pounds was the amount that Mason gave away for public benefit. The man who could hand out such an amount as this at sixty years of age, without feeling it at all, was only worth thirty shillings at thirty years of age. How he became to be a millionaire is almost the same old story. Poverty in youth; integrity in manhood; affluence in old age.

He was left fatherless at twelve years of age, with a widowed mother almost penniless. At thirteen he had not merely to keep himself, but he had to help support his mother and younger brother. School education he had none, and his natural aptitude for business was the outcome of his necessities. He soon found out that to succeed he must depend on himself.

His first work was with a village cobbler, where he, at any rate, was able to keep himself and add a little to his mother's slender store. But the prospect for his future was too limited for the lad; he left it and turned baker for a short while; but this did not suit him, and to obtain larger wages he learnt carpet weaving in Kidderminster. He stopped at this for two or three years, and then went to Birmingham, where there seemed more scope for a youth with some ambition in his soul.

At twenty-seven he went to work for a man who was a large maker of cheap jewellery in Birmingham. He worked hard for this man, and worked conscientiously; hoping to get a higher position in the social scale by gaining his confidence, and becoming manager eventually. In two years he worked himself up past all the other employés, and asked for a large increase of wages. His employer replied by promising him a partnership in a year's time. Mason worked hard, redoubled his energies, and devoted his whole time to the business. Things prospered well with the house.

But he soon received a cruel blow—one that would have permanently dispirited a less resolute man. His employer delayed the promise, then evaded it, and finally broke it at the instigation of his family, when he lay upon what proved to be his death-bed.

Instead of a partnership, Mason was offered a large salary as manager. His open nature revolted at such deception. He refused the offer, and left the place. At the age of thirty, with just thirty shillings as his sole capital, he found himself without

F

employment.   Such a man in such a town as Birmingham had not long to wait.   This cruel incident proved to be the making of his fortune.

He had scarcely left the jeweller's warehouse, still burning with indignation, and suffering from a keen sense of wrong, when an acquaintance met him in the street, and learned the story of his leaving.

"Go to Mr. Harrison, he wants just such a man as you.   Go and see him."   This Mr. Harrison was a split steel ring maker. Mason went straight to him and asked for employment.

"You are not afraid of dirtying your fingers with work?" asked Harrison.

"Try me."

He did try him.   The trial resulted in a permanent engagement and a life-long friendship.   Shortly after, Mr. Harrison made the first steel pen for Dr. Priestly as a novel present.   It was rudely fashioned out of a piece of sheet steel, formed into a tube, and the lower part filed away into the shape of a pen, the part where the tube joined being left as the "split."   Mason happened to see this, and it led to important results.

In the year 1828, Mr. Mason was walking up Bull-street, Birmingham, when, looking into the shop window of Mr. Peart, he saw a card of steel pens marked 3s. 6d. each (much better pens are now sold at fourpence per gross).

"The novelty," said Mr. Mason, recounting the incident afterwards, "and thinking of Mr. Harrison's pen, induced me to go in. Mr. Peart was writing with one of the pens.   He said it 'was a regular pin.'   I instantly saw that I could improve upon it, and bought it for sixpence."   That sixpence was the investment that brought in a million.

On examining the pen, Mason found the name to be "Perry, Red Lion Square, London."   Going home he made three pens, from which he selected the best, and sent it by that night's post to Perry.   A few days afterwards Mr. Perry presented himself in Lancaster-street, Birmingham, to see the man who had made a better pen than his, to ask if he could make them in large quantities, and to conclude a bargain with him.   A bargain was struck, and from this beginning Mason became the largest penmaker in the world.   He soon afterwards invented machinery for stamping, slitting, and grinding.

His name is scarcely known as a penmaker, although he was in the business for fifty years.   The reason is that for many years Perry took all he made, and the pens were all sold with Perry's name.   When he began to make for other dealers he still kept his name back, and stamped his pens with the names of his customers, among which were nearly all the English and many foreign houses.

In 1840 he was quite wealthy, and was looking around for some place to invest his money, when he met Mr. G. R. Elkington, who was then trying to introduce his new system of electroplating. Elkington had everything but capital. Mason had the capital, the insight as to the merits of the invention, and the patience to wait for results. Shortly the grand premises in Birmingham and the firm of Elkington & Mason began to rise, and soon were known to the world. They first tried to grant licences for the new process, and not enter on the manufacture. But the difficulties they encountered compelled them, reluctantly, to begin the manufacture. It was lucky for them that it happened so. Nobody but those actually engaged in the trade believed that it would prove successful, and many of Mason's friends lamented his rashness in risking his capital, and asked him to withdraw from such a hopeless venture. Looking back by the light of present experience, these fears seem ridiculous, but those who know the difficulties of electro-plating in the early days will rate them far more seriously. The new firm had repeated failures and extreme discouragement. But the grand result amply repaid them.

A few years after, Mr. Mason started a new process of copper smelting. He established works at Pembrey, then a small fishing hamlet in Wales; now, thanks to Mason, a flourishing manufacturing town.

Mr. Gladstone offered Mr. Mason the honour of a knighthood, which he accepted. In his successes he did not forget to give liberally to others. He founded a splendid orphanage and a scientific college at a cost of over a third of a million. When his fellow-townsmen were bargaining for a statue to be erected to his honour, he stopped the negotiations, and expressed his disapproval of any such proposal.

SIR GEORGE ELLIOTT,
"THE BONNIE PIT LADDIE."

WHEN a lad begins life at nine years of age, and has to keep himself by slaving down a dirty, dark, coalmine, it seems a hopeless future. When you see that same lad sitting in the parliament of one of the greatest nations of the earth, you naturally suppose that there is something in his history to be worth telling. We propose to explain how the " pit laddie" rose from the position of door-opener to be one of the richest men in the world. His first wages were two shillings a-week; his present wages are £2,000 a-week.

George Elliott was born at Gateshead nearly seventy years ago. His father was a miner, or coalhewer, as it is called. From a collier's cottage to the lordly halls of a baronet and millionaire is a great leap in half-a-century. It is hardly possible to furnish another instance of one who, without having done something to

Leave a name at which the world grew pale,

has at last, by the force of talent and by keeping an eye to the main chance, made himself what Elliott now is.

Sixty years ago a collier's position was one that offered few opportunities for the elevation either of himself or his family. When Elliott was a boy, pitmen in the north had to work 14 hours a-day to eke out a scanty living, and their wages were only four shillings a-day. Elliott's father had a large family, and was compelled to send his sons to work at an early age. When only nine years old he was sent down the pit at Penshaw Colliery as a "trapper," that is, to open and shut the doors giving access to the different sections of the pit. This was not the sort of training to enable a man

To burst his birth's invidious bar.

The trapper has to sit or stand behind a huge door, always in darkness, in the recesses of the mine, and throw it open whenever a passage is demanded for ponies, tubs, or pitmen. There is no opportunity for learning to read, no chance of conversation with his fellows, few facilities for recreation and amusement, nothing suited to the circumstances of a boy. It was in a position of this kind that George Elliott graduated for his distinguished career. It was this very hardship that developed his force of character.

He remained down the pit until nineteen years of age, but the last two years he studied mathematics under two local masters, and made such headway that when he left the grimy pit he was straightway received into a surveyor's office in Newcastle. This engagement proved the first step to his fortune. Close application to business as a draughtsman enabled him to return to the colliery, in six months, as overman. At this time there were many overmen who were very incompetent. It was a rare thing to get one who combined both theory and practice, as Elliott did. His services were rendered very valuable, and he was pretty well paid. But his desire to rise caused him to leave after two years.

His next step upwards was the position of under-viewer at Monkwearmouth Colliery. After two years he was promoted to be head-viewer, having absolute control of one of the largest and deepest pits in England at only 24 years of age. He was the youngest viewer either before or since. At this time, although little more than a youth, his advice was sought by some of the most eminent mining engineers in the country. He had proved himself conversant with every detail of a mine, from the childish duty of trapping up to the sole management. The class of men with whom he now came in contact were large capitalists and noted engineers. The long-headedness of Elliott recommended him to all with whom he did business, and many were the tempting offers he had made to him.

In 1840, when twenty-five years of age, he advised Mr. Russell, of Brancepeth Castle, to buy Washington Colliery, and he would guarantee the venture if one-fourth of the shares were allotted to him. The advice was acted upon; Messrs. Russell, Backhouse, Mounsey, and Elliott held equal interest in the mine. While managing this colliery, he still retained his position as head-viewer of Monkwearmouth Colliery; and, from this date, money began to accumulate fast in his hands. The mine did wonderfully well under his supervision. In three years his capital had increased so, and his credit was so high, that he was able to lease Usworth Colliery—a most extensive undertaking, considering that its total output was 1,200 tons daily.

Being now a large colliery owner himself, he resigned his position at Monkwearmouth, and accepted the appointment of chief consulting and mining engineer to the Marquis of London-derry, who was then developing his estate by forming a shipping port at Seaham Harbour. By Elliott's advice, a pier and break-water were built, the harbour was dredged, and a railroad was built, all owned by the Marquis. In an incredibly short time a large town sprung up as if by magic. Ships resorted to the harbour for coals, and a general merchandise business soon grew up in the town. The town of Seaham Harbour may be said to owe its existence to Elliott.

In 1864 Mr. Elliott's success was so great that he was able to buy the very colliery at which, as a boy, he had acted as trapper. It must have been an interesting sight to see the stylish carriage draw up at the colliery, and the owner alight where a few years before he had stood barefooted, grimy-faced, and tired with his long day's work. It was a moment when any such man might feel proud; for he had raised himself by honest means.

The ownership of Penshaw Colliery was only the stepping-stone to further progress. As soon as it was fairly on the way to yielding good profits Mr. Elliott bought another coalmine—the Powell Duffryn Colliery, in South Wales. He now had three enormous pits, each of which, under his superior management, proved paying affairs. Besides the income from these he made a good income from his position as manager of the Londonderry Estate in Durham. He now had over a thousand men in his employ.

A few years previous to this, however, he had formed a business alliance of a different kind, which proved another means of future distinction. The business of Messrs. Kuper & Co., wire-rope manufacturers, was in process of liquidation, and Mr. Elliott offered to become sole agent for them. In two years he had so reduced the debts of the concern, and made the business pay so well, that he offered to buy the factory, and guaranteed to pay all creditors twenty shillings in the pound and interest, besides a handsome reversion to Messrs. Kuper & Co. The offer was gladly accepted. He next invited Mr. Glass to join him. The new firm of Glass & Elliott rapidly developed the business, and extended it by manufacturing telegraph wires and cables. They were the first to adopt the method of wire covering to marine cables.

They manufactured not only the Atlantic cable, but most of the submarine cables of the world. So successful were they in this particular department that, in 1864, their firm was converted into the world-famous Telegraph Construction and Maintenance Company. The transfer was only partial, so far as Glass & Elliott were concerned, for they still continued to have the largest interest in the company. The manufacture of the Atlantic cable would have made any men famous, but when we consider that they also made the Franco-American, British Indian, and British Australian cables, we are bound to regard Elliott as a wonderful man. They subscribed £400,000 towards the second Atlantic cable, to insure its being built.

The shares of the new company were very soon at a high premium. Mr. Elliott's reputation was spreading in Europe and America. He was now known as one of the most solid business men in the commercial world. But his ambition was far from satisfied. The moneys that he was collecting were re-invested in more coalmines. The tremendous development that all kinds of steam-power was making caused a great demand for coal. Elliott had sufficient foresight to see that there was good property in English coalmines, and he soon purchased two more coalpits in Wales, viz., the Aberaman and the Cwm Noel. He now has about 6,000 men in his employ, and is generally reputed to be worth two million pounds.

In 1868 the electors of the county of Durham threw off their allegiance to the old county families who had hitherto represented them, and sent George Elliott, the " pit laddie," to Parliament, where he has commanded the respect of the House by his strong common sense and his honesty. He received his title of baronet during Mr. Gladstone's ministry, and right well does he sustain the honour of the title.

J. W. MACKEY,

OF CALIFORNIA.

FORTY-FIVE years ago there was a ragged little penniless boy running about the streets of a town in Ireland. The little fellow

was ambitious and adventurous. He had all the native shrewdness of a Milesian and the happy temperament that looks for ever
on the bright side of things. He wanted to go to America, but
had no money to pay his fare. The simplest way of solving such
a difficulty was to steal on board some ship when the cargo was
being loaded. No one noticed the little bit of an Irish waif as he
ran around the ship doing odd jobs for the men, and no one
observed whether he ever left the ship or not. When out at sea a
couple of days he came from his hiding-place, and smilingly offered
to the captain to work his way over. This was the beginning of
a career that brought him in a fortune of fifty millions. The
little stowaway is now the owner of one of the finest palaces in
Paris.

When landed in New York the small Irish boy won his way
into the affections of some of his country people, and he shortly
got work at good wages. He had no time for school education,
all the knowledge he possessed was gained at odd times.

When he was eighteen years of age he invested his savings in a
lot of cheap jewellery and watches, and started out to sell them,
either wholesale or retail. The goods cost him a mere song.
Whenever he got a chance to "trade off" any jewellery for live
stock, he would always do so, and he would drive the animal or
ride it until he could sell it. In this way he gradually made his
way across the settled districts, and found himself on the frontier
of civilisation when the "gold fever" broke out, and every other
man was talking of going to the diggings. Mackey started off
for California, and opened a whisky saloon in San Francisco. The
price for a glass of poor whisky was four shillings, a glass of beer
one shilling. The miners would come in with their gold-dust and
"treat the crowd" all round, then throw down an ounce or two
of dust and ask Mackey to "call it square."

In a short while Mackey was making far more money than the
miners were. He extended his saloon and increased his trade
immensely. The money that he saved was used to buy up
"claims" from men who sickened of the rough life and wanted
to return to "God's country," as the States were called. These
claims he would hold for awhile, and engage men to work them.
If they contained a large amount of "pay dirt" he would keep
them ; if not, he would sell out to some "tenderfoot."

But as he became more wealthy he developed schemes for piling
up the money far faster. One of his plans was to buy a half-
share from some poor prospector, who had spent all his means in
discovering some good mine. The poor man, of course, would have
no capital to develop it, and Mackey's offer of a few hundred
dollars for a half-share, and to furnish the means for working it,
seemed a fair chance. As soon as Mackey got the deed, his rule
was to play the "freeze out" game, that is, refuse to do anything

in the matter—neither do anything himself nor agree to allow anyone else. The result generally was that the needy prospector would tire of waiting, and gladly sell Mackey his half for a paltry hundred dollars or so. In this way he made some scores of thousands of dollars.

As soon as he had frozen out his impecunious partner, he would set men to work and bring out the gold. His men were always paid in his whisky saloon, and unless they willingly spent the most of their earnings with him, he would quickly dismiss them. In this way his wages cost him very little, as the drinks sold at his bar were always the worst that could be obtained, and the prices charged the very highest.

When he was apparently one of the most flourishing men in the new territory, he suddenly became bankrupt, and paid his creditors a mere trifle. All his property was found to have been quietly made over to his wife, and as soon as the bankruptcy proceedings were over, he stood forth as a richer man than ever.

But the great stroke of luck that made this adventurer the rich man that he now is, was the discovery of a silver mine that is literally one mass of ore. It yields him something like two millions a-year in itself. Mr. Mackey has only one child, a daughter, unmarried, and fair to look upon; she is the pet of Paris society, and the envied possessor of innumerable admirers.

JAMES YOUNG,
OF GLASGOW.

EVERYONE has heard of Young's paraffin oil, but few people know that Young was a millionaire, and originally a carpenter. The carpenter's apprentice who entered the night classes of Glasgow University became the President. The poor lad, who first walked into the chemical class clad in clogs and corduroy, gave £10,000 to endow his *alma mater*.

Our hero was the son of a poor struggling joiner, who lived in the Drygate, Glasgow. His father had not the means to give him more than the rudiments of education, and was compelled to take him from school at a very early age to help in the workshop. The lad was naturally a studious boy, and spent his spare time in studying books on chemistry. He eventually put himself under Professor Graham, at the University class, and so distinguished himself in the eyes of his teacher that he received extra attention as an unusually apt scholar.

From the joiner's bench to the chemical classroom was not a natural transition; but Young proved himself equal to it in all respects. When Professor Graham went to the London University to fill the chair of chemistry he wrote for James Young to come and assist him in the laboratory.   Young gladly accepted the position.   This was the first step upwards in a remarkable career.

As assistant to the noted professor of chemistry he not merely advanced his knowledge, he also became acquainted with some noted men—men who were able in after years to give him a lift in his upward course.   Everyone who met Young at this time was struck with his wonderful determination and untiring perseverance. He remained here until about twenty-two years of age, when the management of Muspratt's chemical works, at Newton, near Liverpool, was offered him.   He took the position and remained with them four years.   For the purpose of extending his experience he left and went to Tennant & Co., at Manchester, where he had the sole supervision of the largest chemical works of its kind in the world.   One hundred thousand tons of coals were consumed annually at these works.

When in the University, James Young had made the acquaintance of Dr. Lyon Playfair.   This friendship was the cause of a step being taken that ultimately led on to fortune.   Our hero might have remained a mere manager for others, and the grand secrets that he extorted from Mother Nature might still have lain in the womb of time.

There was a coalmine in Derbyshire in which a spring of oily substance was noticed.   A few years before this the wonderful coal oil from America had been introduced, and was already in great demand.   The owner of the mine had noticed the strong similarity between the substance in his coalpit and the petroleum from America.   He applied to Dr. Lyon Playfair to come and examine it.   Playfair knew the inquiring turn of Young's mind, and felt every confidence in his practical knowledge.   He selected him as the best man to investigate the properties of the wonderful spring.   Young gladly accepted the commission.   On examining the spring he found petroleum dropping from the roof of the mine over the coal.

Believing he had got hold of a good thing, he got a lease of the mine and made extensive preparations for working the petroleum. He had previously recommended his employers to undertake it. They replied that it was too small a thing for them to go into. It was in 1848 that Mr. Young left Manchester to embark on this venture.   He produced two kinds of oil, a thick oil for lubricating purposes, and a thin oil for burning in lamps.

He had given up a good position for this new business, and embarked all his savings in it.   He fully expected to realise a fortune out of this spring.   Tales of millions being got out of American oil-wells fired his imagination, and he was hopeful of starting an industry that would revolutionise the oil trade. Gradually the flow decreased, and none of his efforts to renew it had any effect. At last it "played out" entirely, and Mr. Young was left with a useless mine on his hands, all his savings gone, and many contracts unfulfilled.

It would now have been quite in consonance with the usual style of things if he had given way to dejection, thrown up the sponge, and returned to his position as a mere workman for wages. But the failure of the spring led him to think whether there was no way of making the oil artificially from coal. He reasoned that in all probability the petroleum was the distilled vapour of coal, heated by subterraneous fires, and condensed by contact with the stone above it.

He made numerous experiments for two years, and obtained different products from his trials. The ultimate result was that out of a mixture of cannel coal and soda-ash, heated to steaming point, he got a liquid that contained paraffin. At last he had "struck ile" literally. He knew that there was unlimited supply of very cheap cannel coal, and unlimited demand for burning oil in every part of civilisation. The outcome of his efforts was an immense fortune.

In 1850 he took out patents for his process. In the same year he went into partnership with two other men, and started works at Bathgate, in Scotland, to manufacture coal-oil from cannel or shale. At this time shale was at a tremendous discount. In many places it was thrown out as rubbish ; and at some mines it was an actual loss, as the coalowners paid men to remove it from the pits. In such circumstances Mr. Young was able to place orders at very advantageous prices. His first order was for ten thousand tons at twelve shillings per ton, delivered to his works. In a very few months the price had crept up to thirty shillings, and in a few years it advanced to seventy-five or one hundred shillings.

While his patent lasted, Young had almost a monopoly of the paraffin trade. He made enormous profits. Such rapid strides were seldom heard of in Scotland before. The erewhile youthful joiner was now driving in a carriage and pair, and was buying up vast estates that he foresaw would treble in value in a short while. His old friends were dumbfounded. The little ragamuffin boys with whom he used to fight in the dirty Glasgow closes were now his workmen.

He was not allowed to enjoy undisturbed possession of his monopoly, however. Several firms took advantage of the knowledge that paraffin had been known to a Mr. Reichenbach, previous to Young's patent being issued. One firm after another established works for carrying on the manufacture without regard to Young's patent rights. Against these firms Mr. Young felt himself bound to proceed. In 1854 he obtained a judgment against a Manchester firm for £3,000, and the firm not merely took out a licence for the future, but paid him royalty on the past product of their works. In the next few years he got judgments against three other firms for £27,500, besides royalties on all they had manufactured. All the manufacturers in the kingdom now gladly took out licences from him to work the patent at a royalty of threepence per ton. The whole organisation of competing firms now capitulated, and paid him enormous sums as royalties. He was rolling in wealth. When his patents expired, in 1864, his partnership ended. The works at Bathgate passed into his hands afterwards at a cost of only £50,000. In two years' time he sold them out to a company for £450,000, and was retained as general manager at a large salary. In the meantime Mr. Young started far larger works at West Calder, half-way between Edinburgh and Glasgow. These were situated near to a large supply of shale of very good quality. The works were the most extensive in the country. There were 4,000 acres in the estate, and the oil works covered nearly 40 acres. Young dug his own shale on the estate, converted it into various products, and kept all the profits within his own hands. He produced 120,000 gallons per week, and employed 1,500 men altogether.

This wonderful invention sent up the price of the then most useless coalmines—those in which there was most shale. One mine that Mr. Young bought for £2,000 sold for £200,000 a few months later. It was thus that this huge fortune was made, not merely by the actual profit of the great patent, but by the rapid advance of real estate in consequence, which Mr. Young could foresee would certainly ensue.

The value of the oil produced can be best judged from Dr. Letheby's analysis. He computes that one gallon of Young's oil is equal to one and a quarter gallons of American oil. Mr. Young used to delight in recounting an incident in his voyages up the Mediterranean and the Sea of Azov. He found that in the most out-of-the-way places, where nothing else of English manufacture was sold, he was sure to find "Young's paraffin oil" for sale.

In less than twenty years' time he accumulated a fortune big enough to buy up a dozen rich men, and still leave himself far from poor. After retiring from active business he still continued his researches among the secrets of chemistry. The laboratory at his hall was the recreation ground for his old age. He discovered that to put lime into the lower part of an iron ship would prevent the bilge water from rusting and eating through the iron—a discovery that has saved hundreds of thousands of pounds to the British nation.

JOSEPH PEASE

Was born at Darlington about eighty years ago. His father was a woollen manufacturer ; and after a good schooling near London, young Pease was apprenticed to the firm of which his father was one of the principals. In a short while he rose to be corresponding clerk to the firm.

Such a humdrum beginning as this did not portend in any way the wonderful course that he afterwards pursued. When the common-place-looking Quaker lad was inditing letters in his father's office no one expected that he would ever cause a commercial revolution. Yet he did. He developed the mineral resources of North Yorkshire and South Durham by his railways, and eventually made the whole district subservient to his enterprises. When he began his course of business development the three towns of Stockton, Middlesbro', and Hartlepool only contained 15,000 population in the aggregate; ten years after they had 160,000. Every soul paid tribute in some way or other to the Quaker who first built the railways, and then developed the coal and iron.

There was nothing brilliant about our hero ; no flashes of genius to dazzle the world. He was merely a go-ahead, common-place man, with a good eye to forward his own ends. In all his efforts to improve the commerce of his country he first of all improved his own prospects.

When Joseph Pease came on to the scene of action, great changes were taking place in all kinds of trade and commerce. Inventions of the most revolutionary order were turning old methods topsy-turvy. Luckily for young Pease, his father was a far-seeing man, and helped forward the building of a railway, the first in the world, from Stockton to Darlington. When about thirty years of age Joseph Pease was appointed treasurer to the company. His duties were to negotiate purchases of land and obtain financial support to the undertaking.

One of the strangest difficulties that the new railway had to contend against was to induce mineral owners along the railway to send their coal and iron by it. Pease was almost compelled, against his wish, to buy mines and coalpits just for the purpose of shipping by it, to prove the practicability thereof.

But here he found to his surprise that a wonderful profit lay awaiting him. He discovered that he could send his iron to his coalworks or *vice versa* much cheaper, much quicker, and with less risk. Then he found that he could dig his own coal, carry it to his own ironworks, and get three profits—the profit of an iron mine proprietor, the profit of a railway carrier, and the profit of a coalowner, combined with the extra profit of a smelter. No man could do this without rapidly becoming rich. Pease's money rolled in, and it was all re-invested in railways, mines, pits, coke-ovens, engine-works, or town property.

When about twenty-seven years of age he married Miss Gurney, daughter of the wealthy banker of Norwich. This was the means of bringing him into relationship with very wealthy people, who were able to help him to develop his enterprises. Very soon he was so situated that he could command a hearing in the world of gigantic financiers. His boldest scheme was the Middlesbro' venture.

A lonely house by the seaside, situate on a small estate of freehold land, was bought by himself and a few friends in partnership for a trifling sum of money. He next organised a railway company to build a line to this lonely spot. Then docks were constructed, streets laid out, building sites offered for sale, and large works of all kinds started. Of course the land rose rapidly in value. Pease bought out all his partners, and when unhampered by them he pushed the new town to its utmost capacity, helped to start ship-building, and organised a line of steamers to the continent. He sent his vast mineral productions of both coal and iron to be shipped from the port, and placed a large coal-shipping depôt there.

He next became partner in a pottery works. Then he joined Messrs. Bolckow, Vaughan, & Co., and Messrs. Gilkes, Wilson, and Co. He bought large tracts of ironstone land in Cleveland very cheap, built railways to them, and in this way opened out the new district, which is now teeming with wealth and population. The iron was also carried by his own railway, smelted in his own furnaces, and shipped from his own port in his own steamers. It was a gigantic monopoly, but of an enlightened kind.

Afterwards he leased the Cod Hill mines and built a railway to them. He then went into the business of a fire-brick manufacturer, and invested largely in Stephenson's engine-works at Newcastle.

Joseph Pease was the first Quaker M.P. He positively declined to uncover his head, even in the presence of the Speaker.

JAMES BAIRD,

The Scotch Ironmaster.

James Baird was said to be the wealthiest commoner in Great Britain. He owned magnificent estates that cost him two millions, besides his vast mineral lands and his six great ironworks. The farmer's lad who began life by digging a day-level colliery, and working in it himself, was a few years after employing an army of ten thousand men and boys. His first output of coal in his paltry little pit was a couple of tons a-day. His last output of minerals was something like three thousand tons a-day, at his forty-two blast furnaces, his five or six coalpits, and his limestone quarries.

There was a shelving bank at the foot of a hill near his father's farm, where James Baird made up his mind to try for coal. The farm did not afford sufficient to tempt him to remain at such drudgery as farm life was at that day. So he persuaded some of his brothers to help him, and they opened a small colliery. By living very parsimoniously and working very hard, he was able to make a trifle of money out of his little venture. Collieries were not such valuable property as they are to-day. A man could get a lease of coal-land very cheap before the iron industry had developed. At that time wages were low in the Scotch coal districts. The miners were practically slaves, and were held in a bondage of debt to the masters, from which they seldom freed themselves, except by death. All wages were paid by a truck system, so that the employers were able to make fifty per cent. profit on the goods they compelled the miners to take in lieu of wages.

A year or two after Baird had opened his mine, the demand for coal increased wonderfully. Gasworks were started, iron furnaces were increased, and all kinds of manufactories sprung up in Scotland. Luckily for him he had secured a long lease of the coal-land at very low royalty; while the price of coal crept up his royalty remained the same.

Several valuable inventions in connection with iron smelting were being introduced about 1828 to 1830. One of the most important was a process for smelting iron by hot air instead of mixing the iron with coal. By this plan the iron was much "cleaner," more durable, and brought a higher price when smelted. The process saved time, material, and labour. A Mr. Neilson was the inventor, and as Baird was able to help him in perfecting some of the details, he in return allowed Mr. Baird to manufacture iron under his patent on exceptional terms. This was turning over a new leaf to our hero.

He had been able to save a few hundreds, and by the help of friends he started some small ironworks at Gartsherrie, in partnership with his brothers. None of them were too proud to work at anything that turned up. The Neilson process proved a very profitable method. Like most new industries, the trade were slow to adopt it. Those who, like Baird, could see far enough ahead, reaped a splendid harvest. Wages were very low; trades unions were almost unknown. Iron and coal rose steadily, much faster than wages, and in this way the Messrs. Baird were able to add to their "pile." Each big haul of profits was re-invested in more smelting furnaces. They kept adding to their existing furnaces, more and more, until they shortly had the largest works of its kind in the world, except one.

About this time Mr. Baird noticed the great waste that was all the time going on in the shape of gas and hot air that escaped from the tops of the furnaces. He saw that if he could conduct these down to the furnace to feed the hot-air blast, a very small proportion of heat would then be lost. He tried various devices, but at last hit upon a cupola that quite performed the necessary functions. It was a grand success, and saved an enormous amount of coal.

Baird had now three grand chances to forward his object of becoming a rich man. He had cheap coal royalties, special terms under the Neilson patent, and a startling patent of his own that saved thousands of tons of coal a-year.

He next made up his mind to see if he could not produce a brand of iron that would beat the world. He experimented for months in different directions. He made a visit to the hematite ore mines of Whitehaven, and after patiently studying the qualities, he bought a mine, and bought a ship, and shipped his own ore to Glasgow. By hand-picking all the ore before it was smelted, and by mixing the native with the Cumberland ore, he produced, by his new process, the far-famed Gartsherrie iron, that is so much above the average that the fluctuations of the market scarcely affect it. It is always 10 to 12 per cent. higher than any other brand. From this we may form some idea of the profits. When they bought the large works at Lugar, those at Eglinton, and the equally large works at Portland and Blair, besides the tremendous concern at Muirkirk, they were able to produce over 250,000 tons of iron a-year. But suppose we figure at 200,000 tons. The profits then would be something like a million and a-half sterling.

As Baird's brothers died he was left the sole owner of this gigantic concern, and it is no secret that for years he enjoyed an income of about £800,000.

One of his great inventions was the perfecting of a coal-cutting machine, that was able to do the work of 35 or 40 men. It is driven by compressed air, and is a great labour-saving machine, although not generally adopted because of the opposition of the miners.

ROBERT NAPIER,

OF GLASGOW.

NAPIER's father was a blacksmith at Dumbarton. The old man used to chuckle with glee when his son was among the leading men in Glasgow, as he would remind him that he " was born with the hammer in his hand." The boy was early trained to the same business as his father. After a fair schooling he was regularly apprenticed with his father. His first move, when of age, was to Edinburgh, where he got work under Stephenson, the lighthouse builder and engineer. He always ascribed his experiences here as being the first landmark in his history.

Stephenson found that he had got an ambitious young fellow, with some ability, and he promoted him accordingly. Napier got the highest wages he could, and saved all his spare cash, with a view to starting in business for himself. The blacksmith business does not require a very large capital. A forge, an anvil, and a few tools are his stock-in-trade. When young Napier was twenty-four years of age, he had saved £30 out of his wages, and with this he started business in a little one-storey cottage, in Greyfriars Wynd, Glasgow.

Such a little tumble-down, wretched concern, in which the young man and his two apprentices were barely kept going, did not seem to promise anything very great. The blacksmith, who began life by shoeing horses, became one of the proprietors of the Cunard Line of steamers, and owner of the finest engineering works on the Clyde. The key to his success was "thoroughness." Whatever he did, he did well. Of course there were other qualities that helped to his great fortune, such as shrewdness, integrity, and thrift; but his greatest help was his attention to every detail.

Hard work, laborious days, and very few delights were the means by which Napier qualified himself for rising out of the drudgery of a mere mechanic. For the first three years he was able to do all the work that presented itself, with the help of a couple of boys. But his ambition was to get above the hum-drum anvil of a working blacksmith. Every spare hour was spent in study of some kind or other, generally engineering.

Eventually he got a few odd jobs repairing engines. This work was done so conscientiously that it soon led to other employment in the same line. Napier made up his mind to leave no stone unturned to enable him to become an engine-builder. Each piece of work was a standing advertisement for him. Every man who employed him recommended him to others, and in a few months his little shop was quite inadequate to do all the work that presented itself.

He then ventured to take Camlachie Foundry, where he soon got several contracts of importance. His main trouble now was to get the necessary capital to finish the various contracts as they came in. But a man with the steady habits of Robert Napier soon found favour with some friends, who introduced him to a bank. When the bank saw what manner of man the blacksmith was they supported him. At last he got the contract for the supply of the pipes required by the Glasgow Water Works, and he felt as though there was a better future for him. The profit on this big contract was enough to enable him to enlarge his works by going into engine-building.

The first engine he made was for a small steamer called the *Leven*. Steamers were at this time coming into use, especially for lake and river navigation, and it needed no great penetration to see that in a short while steamers would supersede sailing vessels. This occurred to Napier, and made him pay special attention to this department. But it required careful calculation to be able to compete with the older and richer houses that were better known. He had no one to take him by the hand. He was yet an untried man.

He had what was worth more than a few thousands of capital— he had wonderful confidence in himself, and could afford to wait. He did not have to wait long, for in a few weeks' time the beauty of the new engines that he had put into that little steamer were the talk of the trade, and order followed order in quick succession. In 1826 he got the contract for the engines of the *Eclipse*. These were so much superior to any that had ever been made that his name was at once placed high among the engineers.

A new company was being organised to build steamers, and run them from Glasgow to Liverpool. Now was Napier's golden chance. He took a lot of shares, got himself elected to one of the offices, and secured the contracts for building both the steamers and the engines. All the boats were well built and splendidly furnished. The line of steamers was a grand success, and the shares were soon at a high premium.

This brought Napier into intimate connection with gentlemen in the shipping trade. In this way he was introduced to Sir Samuel Cunard. Sir Samuel broached a plan to Napier that eventually ripened into the largest steamship company in the world. Cunard's idea was to build a fleet of six or eight steamers of 900 tons, for rapid transit to America. Napier at once saw the fallacy of having the ships too small, his proposition was to build them 1,200 tons. Cunard replied that he could not find the money for such costly ships. But by this time Napier was so well known in Glasgow, that his word alone was good for thousands, and he speedily persuaded three friends to go into the new venture, promising for his part to see that the vessels were all properly built and equipped. This was the origin of the renowned Cunard Line. The first four steamers were entirely intrusted to Napier's construction.

There was no looking back after this. His large works were made larger, and as his income increased from steamship owning and engine-building, he re-invested in more steamers, and eventually became the main owner in the Cunard Line.

G

GEORGE MOORE,

THE DRAPER.

ABOUT twelve years ago, the writer was driving through Cumberland, and passed a small shop in a little village at the back of Skiddaw. The name over the door was Moore. He learnt that the little shopkeeper was a relative of the great London draper. Here it was that the future millionaire laid the foundations for his great success by developing his juvenile pugnacity. It was this combativeness of his that secured the fortune he so long enjoyed. As little "Geordie" stood up to his first fight at the village school of Bolton Gate, with the blood trickling from his nose, he little knew it then, but he was practising the very methods which in after life he found so valuable. The story of that fight lingered for years in the records of the boys. His opponent was much bigger than himself, and though the first blow brought the crimson from his nose, he stood up bravely and received his pounding like a little man. He knew he was beaten, but he also knew, and so did his fellows, that he was beaten honourably, without a whimper, by a much bigger boy. That was said to be the only fight he ever lost.

When about fourteen years of age he was apprenticed to a Mr. Messenger, a draper at Wigton. He stayed here four years, and "did his level best," as the Americans say, to please. But he knew that it would be necessary to leave such a town as Wigton if he were ever to climb the social ladder. His first step was to London, where he got a situation in the retail shop of Flint, Kay, and Nicholson, in Soho.

After one year with them he got a situation as warehouseman with the wholesale house of Fisher & Co., of Watling-street. Here he felt as though he had found a chance for his energies, and made up his mind to make himself so useful to his employers that they would be hardly able to do without him. He quickly rose to be town traveller, where he did so well that his firm gave him the first opportunity that presented itself of rising in the house. He next took the Irish journeys, where he was so successful that his salary was raised to £150 a-year. Then he was appointed to the English ground, the best journey the firm had.

It was while on this ground that young Moore made the chance which set him on the high road to fortune. There was a new firm started, called Groucock, Copestake, & Co. Their class of trade was similar to that of Fisher & Co., and their travellers called upon the same customers as Moore. The new firm were young, pushing men, and were gradually building up a nice trade when Moore came on the scene of action. Their head traveller had once grossly deceived Mr. Moore by stealing a march on him under false promises. He and Moore had arranged to start for Liverpool by the same coach one Monday morning, and spend the time together pleasantly. On Saturday night his competitor went down and stole a march on Moore by calling on all the drapers, and securing most of the best orders. Our hero never forgave this man, and resolved to make him remember it. While he was enjoying a supper with his customers, and making fun at Moore's expense, in the hotel at Liverpool, Moore was packing his samples, and started for Manchester by the night coach. He got nearly all the orders in Manchester and left for Leeds, before his rival had fairly recovered from his exultation. From Leeds he pushed on to Newcastle, and from there to Edinburgh and Glasgow, and swept the best orders clean.

From this time forward Moore spared no trouble, no risk, and no time to get ahead of his rival. Copestake's were a good house, but too young to stand any severe competition. He was as strong as a bull, or he could not have stood it. He was a most formidable rival, and all who had to compete with him knew it. No one felt this more than the traveller who had lost the lead at Manchester.

Moore kept up his energy. He took no holidays, but was eternally on the push. Copestake's man found it impossible to make headway against Fisher's traveller, and told his firm so. He advised them to try and get Moore to travel for them. The advice was taken into consideration, and resulted in permission being given to the traveller to offer Mr. Moore a big increase on his present salary.

Of course, Moore saw that he was wanted, but he waited until better terms were offered. The new firm were disappointed at his refusal, and offered a yet higher salary, but still he would not accept it. The senior partner then took the matter up, and personally called on Moore to offer £500 a-year and a guinea a-day for expenses. This was a tempting offer, but luckily for Moore he again refused. He knew what he was worth, and meant to have his price. His reply to Mr. Groucock almost took that gentleman's breath away. He said he had made up his mind not to leave his present employment for anything less than a partnership. This was the last thing that the firm dreamt of offering. It seemed too cheeky for a mere traveller at £150 a-year to coolly talk of a partnership with a large London house. The partners refused to negotiate any longer, and tried to get on without the high-priced young man. They fully expected to have him come around to more reasonable ideas. They waited in vain. Moore went along, still pushing his business, and further injuring their trade.

At last they found it impossible to do without Moore's services, or at least the withdrawal of his opposition. Mr. Groucock again approached him with a higher offer, but to no purpose. He distinctly told them that he had not been working so hard without a purpose, and that purpose was to get a partnership with some good house. Nothing could induce him to abate his demands. They were compelled to agree to his terms. The deed of partnership was drawn up, and in 1830 the house of Groucock, Copestake, Moore, & Co. began to push to the very front of big London houses.

The terms of partnership were that Moore was to have a fourth of the profits for the first three years, and if the partnership was continued after that time he was to have an equal share. He took good care to make his partners quite as anxious as himself for a continuation of the agreement. Wherever he went the same success awaited him. The trade of his firm developed fast, and soon he found that the house of which he was a member was rapidly assuming a position second to none in the world.

At the end of the three years his partners gladly took him in as equal partner, and now, at twenty-seven years of age, he married the daughter of one of the largest retail drapers in London.

His business continued to grow steadily, but such work as he had been doing had gradually undermined his health. He was advised to take a rest and travel for his health. In 1844 he crossed the Atlantic by the *Great Western* steamer for New York, and true to his usual habits, pushed their trade in America until their American connection was vastly extended. He found that there was a profitable business to be done in English laces among the people who had recently acquired wealth in the New World. As soon as he returned he advised his partners to build a lace manufactory at Nottingham. This was done, and it led to the development of their business to such an extent that branches were shortly established at Manchester, Paris, New York, Philadelphia, and Newcastle.

The trade still continued to increase under the pushing energies of the three partners. When Mr. Groucock died in 1851, Moore's position in the firm was much advanced. He became literally the moving spirit of the whole concern. After a few more years, when he felt that he had secured a fortune large enough for all reasonable requirements, he turned his thoughts to the little village among the Cumberland hills, and bought for £40,000 the mansion of Whitehall, at which he used to gaze with almost worshipping eyes as a rude country lad. Now he entered it as its proud owner. The first person to greet him as he entered its portals was the old dame who acted as lodge-keeper. She extended her hand in the true spirit of equality, and reminded George "that for years they sat upon the same bench at the village school." Mr. Moore always said that hearty welcome in the true Cumberland style did him more good than medicine; it brought back the feelings that, among the rush of London, he seemed to have lost, and for a time he was the happy lad who derived more pleasure in the pursuit of wealth than he ever had in the ownership of it.

Mr. Moore repeatedly refused to be nominated for Parliament. When elected to the honour of Sheriff for the City of London, he paid the penalty of £500 rather than serve. Nearly every charity in London benefited by George Moore's liberality.,

---

In writing these sketches, we have been struck by the similarity of method which each millionaire has adopted to become rich. The only secret of their methods has been hard work in starting life, and dogged perseverance when once started.

George Peabody, when addressing a school of boys, once said that every boy before him could become as wealthy as he was. That statement needs qualifying. There is not wealth enough in the world for every man to be rich. It follows as a necessity, that some must be poor if others are to be millionaires. If all the money in the world were equally divided, there would be about £100 for everybody. If a few hundred men get hold of a million each, some one must have less than his share.

We estimate the number of millionaires in the world at 700, divided about as follows :—

United Kingdom	200
America	100
Germany	100
France	75
Russia	50
India	50
Other countries	125

Statistics as to a man's wealth are most difficult to obtain. His friends usually exaggerate the value of his property until they come to prove the will, when their tone changes. They sadly under-estimate the amount when they have to pay the probate duty of so much per cent. Very few millionaires know their actual wealth, as much of it is dependent on fluctuations of the market.

Most of the gigantic fortunes have been made since the introduction of steam-power, and nearly all have been increased, directly or indirectly, by that agency. A few very large fortunes have been made by banking and several by trading, while a few have simply grown up by the "unearned increment" of land increasing in value. But the young millionaires have got their millions mainly by manufacturing and by railways.

Most of the large fortunes of the world have been made within the last forty years.

Jay Gould made his by stock-gambling and railway building.

Mackey got his in California by lucky discoveries of gold and silver mines. He is an Irishman, and 20 years ago was a bankrupt.

The Rothschilds made theirs by financing.

Vanderbilt's fortune was made by an old canal boatman who

used to own a boat on the Hudson River. He was the first to appreciate the importance of ferry steamers.

Jones, "the silver king" of Nevada, secured his millions by "striking it rich" in a silver mine.

The Duke of 'Westminster increased his wealth to its present colossal proportions by selling land for building purposes in London on short leases.

Jacob Astor must date his rise from the extension of the city of New York, thereby increasing enormously the value of his properties.

William Stewart was the son of a Presbyterian clergyman in the North of Ireland. He was the richest draper in America. His widow still carries on the business.

James Gordon Bennett owes his riches to his enterprise as a newspaper proprietor.

The Duke of Sutherland is rich because his vast estates in the north of Scotland have increased in value through the great improvements of the last thirty years.

The Duke of Northumberland from the same cause.

The Marquis of Bute made his money by the growth of the town of Cardiff, in which he owns nearly all the land.

The various amounts are necessarily approximate estimates only, based on the most reliable authorities.

	Capital.	Income.	Per Month.	Per Day.	Per Hr.	Per Minute.		
	£	£	£	£	£	£	s.	d.
Jay Gould	55,000,000	2,800,000	233,000	7,700	320	5	6	8
Mackey	50,000,000	2,500,000	200,000	7,000	300	5	0	0
Rothschild.........	40,000,000	2,000,000	170,000	5,600	230	4	0	0
Vanderbilt.........	25,000,000	1,250,000	104,000	3,460	140	2	6	8
Jones, the Silver King	20,000,000	1,000,000	80,000	2,700	110	2	0	0
Duke of Westminster	16,000,000	800,000	66,000	2,200	90	1	10	0
John Jacob Astor	10,000,000	500,000	40,000	1,300	50	0	16	0
Stewart	8,000,000	400,000	33,000	1,100	46	0	15	0
J. Gordon Bennett	6,000,000	300,000	25,000	830	33	0	11	0
Duke of Sutherland	6,000,000	300,000	25,000	830	33	0	11	0
Duke of Northumberland	5,000,000	250,000	20,000	700	30	0	10	0
Marquis of Bute...	4,000,000	200,000	17,000	550	23	0	7	0

These calculations, under each heading, are not fractionally correct. We simply wish to present a table giving an idea of the enormous fortunes, so that anyone can at a glance learn the interesting details thereof.